Wife 101

Wife 101

A'ndrea J. Wilson

Divine Garden Press

Soperton, Georgia

Printed by Createspace
Published by Divine Garden Press
Soperton, Georgia 30457

ISBN-13: 978-1466298750
ISBN-10: 1466298758

Cover Photograph: © Zhelobkov/Dreamstime.com

Cover Design: A'ndrea J. Wilson

To the Father, the Son, and the Holy Spirit, which are One. It's not about me; it is all for You, so have Your way in me.

Acknowledgements

Thank you to my mother, Pastor Kathleen Wilson for your seeds of love, faith, and support. To my friends and family that have helped me along this journey; I love you all. Special thanks to Tanisha Smith, Kesha Wilson Lee, Carmen Calhoun, Sharon Bruner, and Darius Harmon. To my editor, Adele Brinkley, for your heart and professionalism. To the Divine Garden Press Family, let's make a difference with the words that we write; the world needs more than just entertainment. To my sisters, Zeta Phi Beta Sorority, Inc. – Chi Pi Zeta Chapter, the Candler County Bookclub, and Christian Authors on Tour. Shout outs to Zetas and Sigmas worldwide, and peace to the Divine Nine. Much love to my hometown Rochester, New York, and all of my childhood friends; you know who you are. To every author whose books I have read and learned from. To the published authors who have lent me their ears and imparted wisdom upon me during the construction and preparation of this manuscript: Mary Monroe, Laura Castoro, Kendra Norman-Bellamy, Norlita Brown, and Vanessa Davis Griggs. To my photographer, Antonio Cleveland; thanks for always looking out for me. To OOSA Bookclub and Ms. Toni for your encouragement on the first novel; I hope you enjoy this one too. To the readers, whose support I value immensely; without you this book would be pointless. Most importantly, to the Great I Am for Your endless love, consistent presence, and needed salvation. I write to please, honor, and glorify You. Thank You for one more opportunity to serve You.

Lesson 1: The Reason Why He Won't Marry You

Therefore a man shall leave his father and his mother and shall become united and cleave to his wife, and they shall become one flesh.

(Genesis 2:24)

I knew; I just knew when Chris called me up and invited me out for lunch on Tuesday that he wanted me back. I had been a terrific girlfriend to him for over a year, and after the way we broke up, how he just fell off the face of the earth, I was certain that one day he would come crawling back, begging for my forgiveness.

I was right about one thing: he wanted my forgiveness. But I was completely wrong about him wanting me back. Instead, the truth of his reappearance slapped me across the face like a greedy, old pimp (well, not literally).

"I'm getting married!" he announced with glee as if I should be happy for him.

I raised my right eyebrow in response. It was the only thing I could do to refrain from strangling him. I wanted to smile, not because I liked what he was telling me, but just so that I could pretend as if what was left of my broken heart wasn't shattering into a million pieces and blowing away. Unfortunately, the pseudo smile ended up looking more like I had swallowed a box of Lemonheads candy.

"Amber, are you okay?" he asked sympathetically as he noticed my sour expression.

In my mind, I went off. *What do you mean, "Am I okay?" Seriously? We just broke up like three months ago, and now you're claiming that you're getting married? And technically, we didn't breakup; you just stopped returning my calls! It's January; you stopped communicating with me in October! So, is this why you disappeared? Were you cheating the entire time we were together? Did you leave me for her? And what, after all of your indiscretions, do you want a cookie or some kind of congratulations from me because you're getting married?*

Okay, I wish I would have said all of that, but what I really said was, "I'm fine. So...married, huh?"

He grinned like the Cheshire Cat. "Yeah. Can you believe it?"

"Not really. Who is she?"

I thought his smile couldn't get any bigger, but somehow it did. "Her name is Noel. She is so amazing! I really think you'd like her."

No, I already hated her. What was wrong with this dude? Why was he doing this to me? I sighed deeply because I could feel the ugly getting ready to come out of me and ransack the uppity restaurant, pulling patrons out of their seats, knocking water glasses over, and shutting down that annoying stereo system that was playing the worst elevator music I had ever heard. "I see...Chris. Not to be funny or anything, but why are you telling me this?"

He shook his head as if he understood my question. Then reached across the table, grabbed my hand, and squeezed it gently. He looked directly into my eyes before replying. "I'm sorry. I know I'm not doing this the right way. Listen, it was wrong the way I left things between you and me. I shouldn't have walked out on you like that; I-I didn't know what else to do. It wasn't working, and I felt like I needed my space. So I went out-of-town for a couple weeks to visit some family up north, and while I was there, I met Noel. Everything happened so fast; I really wasn't expecting to fall in love. I know this is the right thing to do, that Noel is my soul mate, but I really felt that before I married her that I needed to first make things right with you."

If this scene had been one of my fantasies, that moment would have been the time when I would have thrown a drink (preferably something red) in his face and stormed off. However, it was reality, so I just smiled weakly and nodded.

"I hope you can forgive me for the way I treated you. I apologize from the bottom of my heart," he stated passionately as he began to rub my captured hand.

I politely pulled my hand away from him. Although I wasn't ready to hear any more truths, I had to know how he could marry someone else so easily. "Tell me something, Chris. We dated for over a year, and you never wanted to talk about marriage, but you've been dating Yuletide for less than three months, and you are already engaged? I don't understand. Was I really that bad of a girlfriend?" I felt that knot in my throat, the one I usually got before tears overtook my face. *Please don't cry*, I mentally pleaded with myself.

Now avoiding eye contact, he sat back in his seat. "Uh, it's Noel, not Yuletide. And no, you weren't a bad girlfriend per se, you were just...you know..."

"Say it. I won't get mad."

A heavy sigh escaped his lips. "Too independent."

My eyes widened. "What are you talking about? What are you saying?"

He made eye contact again; seemingly ready to lay out all of his cards on the table. "I'm saying that you wanted to be both the man and the woman in the relationship, but where did that leave me? What role was I supposed to play?"

My jaw dropped in shock. "That is so untrue!"

He signaled for the waiter to bring the check as he pulled his wallet out of his back pocket. "You asked. I am simply being honest. Amber, you're a good woman, and you have a lot to offer. You're smart and beautiful, things that men are looking for in a mate, but for future reference, next time you meet a good man, let him be the man."

Ouch! What was that supposed to mean?

Lesson 2: Your Friends (Especially the Single Ones) Don't Know Anything!

There is a way that seems right to a man and appears straight before him, but at the end of it is the way of death. (Proverbs 14:12)

"I can't believe he said that mess to you!" my best friend Tisha exclaimed. Although she was on the other side of the phone and invisible to me, I was sure that Tisha was pacing the floor like she always did when she was hyped.

I was on my way back to work following my disastrous lunch with Chris and didn't waste any time calling "my girl" to tell her what happened. Driving aggressively down I-85 South through downtown Atlanta, I connected my Bluetooth earpiece so I could talk freely while I battled one o'clock traffic.

Replaying Chris' words in my mind, I sucked my teeth, irritated by his accusations. "Me neither! First of all, I'm not trying to be a man, I am just being me! And secondly, what is so wrong with being independent? Men are always complaining about gold diggers and claiming they want a woman who can stand on her own two feet, but when they get one, they say you're too independent! I don't get it! Make up your mind, dude!"

Ten minutes later, I pulled my black Cadillac Escalade into the parking lot of my pastry shop. Sweet Tooth Oasis was only one of the businesses I owned. I also owned a small real estate company, Amber Ross Realty, and a 24-hour daycare, Sunrise Sunset Daycare. "Owned" was the correct term. With the exception of the realty company, I didn't work at them or even handle their operations. I was an investor who knew how to create new businesses from nothing and then put them into the hands of qualified employees to maintain. A few times a month, I would make my rounds, check the books, and ensure that everything stayed afloat. I did, however, have a work office at Amber Ross Realty, which I used to conduct business and meet with various associates, thereby causing me to spend more time there than anywhere else. I was already considering a new business, a natural foods grocery store, but it would mean more money and possibly entering into a partnership, something I was extremely hesitant about doing. I parked my truck in a handicapped space and let out a frustrating sigh.

Tisha, picking up on my exasperation, responded with the typical single female rebuttal. "They make me sick! You know what it is, right? He is clearly intimidated by you."

Turning the key, I shut off the vehicle's engine. "Probably...He kept bringing up that chick Peace, Joy–whatever her name is!" I pulled the key out of the steering column and tossed it into my purse. "She must be one of those needy females. I guess that's what he really likes."

Tisha huffed. "Just trifflin'. Anyways, how did the conversation end?"

"He paid for the check and invited me to his engagement party this weekend."

"What?" Tisha yelled. "You've got to be kidding me!"

"Seriously. That's what he said. But I don't want to go to that foolishness! What would I look like showing up to his engagement party when he is marrying some other woman?"

"Well, I think you should go."

"Are you crazy?"

"No! Don't worry; I'll go with you." Tisha got quiet for a second, probably imagining the scene in her mind, and then continued. "Yeah, we should go. You should go looking hot and take a date, someone fine! When he sees you looking sexy and hanging on another guy's arm, he will be so jealous. He'll dump Miss Thing in a heartbeat."

I watched two of my employees carry a sheet cake out to a customer's car and load it into the backseat. "Where am I supposed to get this fine date? I don't have a bag of good looking men that I can simply pull out of on a whim!"

"Hire one."

I gasped. "What? Like an escort? No way!" My employees heard me yell out and glanced over at my truck. I waved politely to let them know that everything was okay and to keep it moving.

Tisha giggled. "Why not? It's not like you're paying him for sex; you're merely using him for his company. Men do it all the time."

"Yeah, but…I…I don't know. Isn't it kind of desperate to hire a date?"

"No one will know you paid him except us. And you are not trying to really be with him, you're only using him to make Chris jealous. It is purely for show. Matter-of-fact, I know someone you can use!"

I groaned. "What? Who?"

"Don't worry about it. Text me the details about the party, and I will make sure that we enter the place with the most beautiful men in town."

I opened the truck door and slid out of the seat, grabbed my bag, and slung it over my left shoulder. "Okay, you have got me a little nervous, but I'm going to trust you on this one. Let me go run in here and pick up this box of paperwork, and I will call you later."

After Tisha said goodbye, I pressed end on my cell phone and tucked it into my purse. I had a feeling that going along with Tisha's plan wasn't the right move to make, but at the same time I did want to see Chris squirm. I shrugged off my concerns, pushed my shoulders back, and walked towards the employee entrance of the bakery. Time to go back to work.

Saturday evening seemed to come before I could blink twice. My work week had been so busy that I hadn't had the chance to discuss further with Tisha the men who were supposed to be accompanying us to the engagement party. In my brief conversations with her, she told me that she had everything covered, and I was forced to believe her.

Like me, Tisha was a self-made woman. With a Master's degree in education, she was a vice principal at one of the local high schools and being considered for the principal position when the current principal retired at the end of the school year. Tisha and I had been roommates during our junior and senior years in undergrad at Emory University in downtown Atlanta, Georgia. We had so much in common that our friendship continued beyond college, through our twenties, and into our thirties. Tisha, the studious out of the two of us, went onto graduate school while I jumped head first into the work world.

Using my Bachelor's degree in business administration, I worked a few entry level corporate jobs, which I hated, while I saved my cash. Five years after graduation, I had enough money put away to buy my first house and invest in my first business, the realty company. I became a licensed real estate agent and then a broker and opened my agency. I held on to my nine-to-five for three more years as I saved more money to open the daycare. My real estate business was doing well and able to cover its own expenses, so by the time I opened my daycare, I was able to quit my daytime job and focus solely on my investments. By the time I reached thirty-one, I had two businesses, a residential house, and a rental property, and was working on plans for the pastry shop. Yes, I was indeed driven.

Still wondering who would escort me to the engagement party, I slid on a new gold, off-the shoulders, satin blouse and a pair of black, wide leg dress pants. After sweeping my naturally curly hair into a simple up do, I applied some eye shadow, eyeliner, lip gloss, and mascara to my face, eased into a pair of trendy, gold pumps, threw a black shawl over my shoulders, and headed over to Tisha's place.

I rang the doorbell of Tisha's two story, red brick house with black shutters. A tall, sexy, dark-skinned Adonis with a dimple in his right cheek answered the door comfortably, as if he had lived there his whole life. "You must be Amber," he said seductively before I could even get my thoughts together to ask him who he was and why he was answering my best friend's door.

"Yeah, and you are?" I asked with a hint of an attitude.

He smiled, making the dimple in his cheek deeper. "Lenny, but most people call me Rude Boy."

As attractive as he was, I was not impressed. "Uh, yeah. I think I'll stick with Lenny. Is Tisha here?"

He backed away from the door to allow me to enter. "She's getting ready. Come on in."

I walked into my best friend's house as if it was the first time I had ever seen it, peering around each corner, looking for any other surprises. Entering the living room, I found what I was seeking. Another handsome guy, also with dark skin and an amazing body, leaned back on the sofa and gazed intensely at the TV that was playing a recap of a football game from Sunday. Noticing I had come into the room, he briefly glanced up, nodded his head at me in acknowledgement, and then refocused back on the game.

At that moment, I heard the clacking of Tisha's stilettos as she walked down her hardwood stairs and entered into the living room. "Hey girl!" she screamed as she walked toward me to give me a hug. "You look gorgeous!" she complimented before pulling me into her embrace. "Yes, this is what I am talking about! Chris is going to faint when he sees you. I can't wait to see his face."

"Yeah, well, we'll see about all that," I responded, uncertain Chris falling head-over-heels for me would be the outcome of the evening. "You look good too! I love those shoes!" I exclaimed as I favorably scanned her yellow strappy shoes that had little gold chains wrapped around the ankles and 3-inch skinny heels.

She struck a flirty pose like a fashion runway model. "Thanks! So have you met our dates?"

I looked at the two men who were both engrossed in the sports highlights. "Kind of, not really."

"Well Rude Boy, I mean, Lenny will be escorting you, and Gary will be my date," she said as she pointed out who was who.

Hearing their names, they turned to look at us. I grabbed my friend's arm and said under my breath, "Can I talk to you in private for a second?"

"Okay," she responded to me and then glanced over at the men. "Fellas, we'll be right back."

We walked out of the living room into her lemon yellow painted, enclosed kitchen. Her shoes seemed to clack even louder as she crossed the pearl-white tile floor and stopped in front of the refrigerator. "What's up girl? Aren't they fine?" she boasted.

I rolled my eyes in irritation. Yes, they were good looking, but something was off about the whole thing. "Rude Boy? Are you for real? Where did they come from? And what kind of name is Rude Boy? Sounds like, like a stripper's name or something!"

She laughed. "They like to be called exotic dancers."

It took everything in me not to grab her and shake the stupid out of her. Panicking, but still aware of the men in the other room, I replied in a loud whisper, "What? Oh-my-gosh! No, Tisha! I am not showing up to Chris' engagement party with a stripper!"

Tisha mocked my tone. "Yes you are! He is perfect. Chris won't know he's a stripper, but he will notice how much more of a man Lenny is than he ever was."

I threw my hands up in surrender. "I can't believe I let you talk me into this."

"Girl, chill out! It's going to be fine; trust me," Tisha concluded.

I should have run at that very moment. I wish I had run, but no, I stayed. Trusting my harebrained best friend, I stayed and showed up at that engagement party with Lenny a.k.a. Rude Boy the Exotic Dancer.

The night was a complete flop. It didn't go at all as planned or imagined. First, Chris was a little surprised to see me with Rude Boy, but jealous? Not at all. He was so wrapped up in his brown-skinned beauty that he couldn't have cared less whom I showed up to the party with. I could have been there with President Obama, and Chris wouldn't have looked twice. He was really into his woman, which made me feel even worse. Engagement parties are hard enough to swallow when you're single and want to be married, but they are even tougher to digest when the groom is your recent ex. If I had to watch one more second of him softly caressing her back or endure one more "awe" provoking kiss because someone thought it would be cute to clink their silverware against their wine glass, I was going to vomit.

Second, being on a date with a stripper is worse than standing in line at the Department of Motor Vehicles. Their lives are vain, filled with dancing for money and fulfilling sexual fantasies. He had absolutely nothing to talk about. I mean honestly, how many times a day can one person spend working out and thinking about doing the nasty? Ugh! Then to make matters worse, he tried to hit on me! Talking about I'm his for the night, we can do whatever turns me on, and he can tell that I like a man who does this and that. I quickly set him straight and told him that I was paying for him to shut up and look good, that was all! I didn't want sex or anything else including a conversation from him. *Lord, why me?*

By the time I got in my bed that night (alone!), I was hurt, frustrated, angry, annoyed, and tired. No more listening to Tisha (I've said that one before). I had to do something different because my relationships were just not working. My love life was a mess, and I didn't understand why. I knew that I was a wonderful woman with a lot to offer a man, but somehow every guy I dated couldn't see it. Was Chris right? Were men turned off because I wouldn't let them be the man? And really, what did that even mean? I silently prayed, asking God for understanding and help in the romance department. Church was most definitely on Sunday's agenda. Based on the way my life was going, I needed some serious divine intervention.

Lesson 3: Align Yourself with Wise Women Who Can Edify You

He who deals wisely and heeds [God's] word and counsel shall find good, and whoever leans on, trusts in, and is confident in the Lord–happy, blessed, and fortunate is he. (Proverbs 16:20)

There is a common adage, "God is an on-time God!" I can surely testify, "Yes, He is!" By the time I rolled up into church on Sunday morning, I was certifiably depressed. I'd cried all night and all morning, barely able to shower and dress, but after listening to a few songs from the Christian radio station, I was encouraged enough to pull myself together and make it out to the House of God. I didn't wear any makeup because the way I was feeling, I was certain to be in tears by the time the choir sang their first heart-stirring ballad. Surprisingly, I made it through the service with dry eyes and peace in my spirit. I was too busy enjoying the rhythmic beat of the drums, charismatic style of the pastor, and warm embraces from the members to be burdened down with sobs and sadness.

The service came to a heighten peak when a petite, 40's-something woman went to the podium prior to the preaching segment to give a special announcement. I had seen her around the church before, but being a sporadic churchgoer who rarely participated in supplementary activities related to the ministry, I had no idea who she was or what her position in the church was.

"Praise the Lord, Saints," she began. Her welcome was followed by head nods, waves, and a congressional, "Praise the Lord" response.

"As many of you know, we are starting a new ministry in the church to address concerns about Christian dating and marriage. There are a lot of single people who wish to be married, but are finding it difficult to meet the right person or are struggling with maintaining the relationship once they meet someone special. There are also a lot of married individuals who are in need of the skills and tools to overcome many of the challenges associated with marriage.

"In response to many questions about relationships, we have created a series of personal development training courses for men and women. Our first courses will commence tomorrow night and will include the classes Wife 101 and Husband 101. We would like to invite any single or married people who want to learn more about how to be more effective in their relationships to come out at 7 p.m. The ladies will meet in our fellowship center, and the men will meet in the choir room. There is a signup list in the rear of the church. We ask that if you are interested that you please sign up before you leave church today so that we have a good idea of how many people to expect tomorrow. Thank you for your time and be blessed."

A chorus of "Amens" followed her departure from the pulpit.

I watched the woman attentively as she made her way back to her seat in the second row. As the service continued, I found myself unintentionally staring at her. Questions swirled through my mind about the classes on relationships and whether or not I should attend. I felt as if God had heard my plea and wanted me to participate, but I was unsure and, therefore, a bit reluctant. I wanted to know more about how I should deal with men and what God expected from me, but then again, I didn't want a bunch of religious folks telling me to wear long skirts and stay barefoot and pregnant. Nonetheless, my interest was stirred, and I was willing to test the course out, at least the first class. *If I don't like it, I'll just stop going.*

Following the benediction, I stopped by the signup table in the rear of the church. By the time I got to the signup sheet, ten other women had already scribbled down their names. I peered over at the men's sheet and noticed that it also had six or seven signatures. *Hmm... I guess I'm not the only one who needs a love makeover.* Confidently, I added my name to the list and headed towards the exit.

As my hand touched the handle on the exit door, I felt a tap on my right shoulder. I instantly turned around and came face-to-face with the petite announcement lady. *Had she caught me staring at her during service?* I wondered, but before I could entertain that thought any further, she explained her approach.

"Hi. I'm Lydia Woods. I noticed that you signed up for the class tomorrow and just wanted to introduce myself. I will be teaching the women's course, and my husband, Minister Martin Woods, will be teaching the men's class."

"Oh," I said with a slightly forced smile.

"Are you married?" she asked politely. "If so, please invite your husband as well."

I shook my head. "No, I'm not married. I'm single."

A sincere smile spread across her face. "Well that's okay. We want to provide information that both single and married woman can benefit from. Do you have any questions about the class?"

I pulled my purse up further on my arm and unconsciously began to rub my fingers against the leather strap. I fidget when I'm nervous. *Why was I nervous?* "Uh…I don't know…um…I guess…what will we be doing?"

"This is the first course on the topic so I thought it would be suitable to start with studying Proverbs 31. Once we complete this course, we are hoping to start a second class in which we will study other lessons in the Bible on wifehood. Just bring your Bible, a pen, and a writing notebook, and I am certain God will have something wonderful to teach you. Oh, if you have any questions as the class progresses, you can call me anytime." She passed me a small slip of paper with her name and number written on it. "I look forward to seeing you tomorrow, Sister…?"

I stuffed the paper in my purse. "Ross. Amber Ross." *Did I think I was James Bond or something?* After a moment of awkward silence, I mumbled, "Thanks. I guess I will see you tomorrow." I smiled respectfully, turned, and quickly headed out the door.

Lesson 4: Be Someone He Can Take Home to His Momma

The words of Lemuel, King of Massa, which his mother taught him: What, my son? What, son of my womb? What [shall I advise you], son of my vows and dedication to God? Give not your strength to [loose] women, nor your ways to those who and that which ruin and destroy kings. (Proverbs 31:1-3)

Monday evening, following a draining workday of having needed repairs done at the daycare, I returned to church for the Wife 101 course. Still a little skeptical, I hadn't told any of my friends about the class. Although most of my friends were Christians and educated, they weren't the most open minded group of people. I could just hear Tisha saying, "I don't need to take a class to teach me how to keep a man. There's nothing wrong with me; it's these lame, good-for-nothing men that need a class! 'How to Get Your Life Together and Be a Real Man.' Now, that's a class they should offer!" No, I would have to venture this class alone, unlike the other women in the class who were obviously sharing the experience with close friends. Before class started, they comfortably chattered away about multiple topics from work to weddings, making me feel completely like the oddball, the disconnected soul.

At 7 p.m. sharp, Announcement Lady, better known as Lydia, stood in front of the small group of twelve women, causing everyone to become silent. "Okay, ladies. We are going to get started," she said cheerfully. "My name is Lydia Woods, and I will be the facilitator for Wife 101. In this course, we are going to explore the role of a wife from the biblical perspective and apply these truths to contemporary society and lifestyles. Before we get started with our first lesson, let me tell you about myself, and why I've been given the task of teaching this class."

Lydia cleared her throat before continuing. "I got married when I was 28 years old. My husband is a minister here at the church, and we have been married for 20 years now. We have three children, two girls and a boy. Our oldest child recently graduated from high school last year and is now in his second semester of college. Our two girls are still in high school. They are in the 10th and 11th grades.

"Before I got married, I went to college and got a Bachelor's and Master's Degree in biology. I started working as a Science Researcher for the Center for Disease Control during the day and teaching college courses at night at Georgia Perimeter College. I was making a lot of money for a woman in her mid-twenties, and I felt successful.

"Then I met my husband. At the time he was working at a factory, and although he made a decent salary, I made significantly more than him. I wasn't that into him initially, but he was determined to make me his wife, and eventually I fell in love with him. We got married and immediately, I got pregnant. I had a lot of complications with my first pregnancy and couldn't work, so I quit my teaching job and took a leave of absence from my day job at the CDC. When our son was born, he was a very sickly child who required a lot of care. I was scared to leave him with anyone, so I ended up permanently leaving my job with the CDC to care for my son. After he turned two, he was a lot healthier, but I was pregnant again so I still couldn't go back to work. It seemed like every time I wanted to re-enter the job force, something major happened in my life that prevented me from returning.

"By the time I was ten years into my marriage, I accepted the fact that God didn't want me to work, but wanted me to be at home with my family. I received so much criticism from others because I didn't work outside the home. It was difficult to have to explain myself to others and being frowned upon, but God had a plan for me. A couple years ago, I went back to school and through distance learning I earned a second Master's, this time in Biblical Studies. Since then I have been conducting workshops and seminars related to family life from the Christian perspective. And now I am here today with you; to teach you about your role as a woman, wife, and mother."

Lydia looked around the room and made eye contact with each of us. "The purpose of Wife 101 is to give you some basic information about your role as a woman and to help you understand God's purpose for your life. There are many ideas about what a woman should or shouldn't do and about how she fits into the family unit. By the end of this class, it is my hope that you will embrace your purpose as a wife or future wife, as well as be in a better place spiritually to follow God's leading as it relates to your romantic relationships."

She walked over to the table in front of the room and picked up a medium sized, brown, leather covered bible, and then continued. "Wife 101 will focus on the study of the virtuous woman or Proverbs 31. We will break down this chapter verse by verse to have a richer understanding of what the word is trying to tell us about our role as women. Everyone, take out your bibles and turn to Proverbs 31 and read verses one through nine. I will be teaching from the Amplified bible, but whatever version you have will be fine for you to use."

Everyone in the class, including me, shuffled through her belongings, took out their bibles, and flipped to the thirty-first chapter of Proverbs. I quietly read the first nine verses quickly and then read them again slowly to make sure I hadn't missed anything. A minute after I completed my second reading, Lydia began to speak again.

"Our first lesson deals with the first nine verses of the chapter. Often when people read or talk about the virtuous woman in Proverbs 31, they skip over the first nine verses. Those of us who have studied the bible know that the context in which verses are written is very important to the meaning of them. Therefore, it is imperative that we look at verses one through nine." Some of the women in the room nodded in agreement.

"For those of you who are mothers already, think about your children. If you have a son, think about him. If you don't have children or don't have a son, imagine that you had a son. Imagine that this son was at the age where he wanted to date and even get married. Now imagine that he was willing to sit down with you and allow you to give him advice concerning the type of woman that he should date and marry. What would you tell him? He is listening and willing to hear anything you want to tell him about women, dating, and marriage. Specifically, what traits would you tell him to look for in a wife? These are rhetorical questions, but just think for a second about what you would want to tell your son."

Looks of surprise and uncertainty filled the faces of the women in the room, me included. *How would I describe a good woman to my son? I'm not sure, but I do know one thing I would tell him: Leave the airheads alone.*

Lydia gave us a few more seconds to think then began to speak again. "Now, let's up the ante. Not only is this your son, but you are the queen of your country, your husband has died, and your son is now the king of the land! Not only do you want your son to have a good wife because you want the best for your son, but who he chooses as a wife will be the next queen! She will impact both him and the nation. Now, what traits and qualities would you advise your son to look for in a wife?"

Definitely leave the airheads alone. And get a woman who's more than just pretty. Trophy wives aren't worth the Gucci bags they parade around clutching.

"Verses one and two teach us that this chapter is a collection of wisdom given to King Lemuel by his mother who wants to lead him in the right direction. Notice that she begins by asking, 'What do I say; what do I tell you?' Even though you all did not speak out loud your answers to what you would tell your sons, like this mother, I am sure you felt the same way. How do you even begin to give out this kind of advice? So much needs to be said, but where do you start?

"When she does figure out her thoughts and begins to give him guidance, the first thing she says is 'Give not your strength to women.' The Amplified version says, 'Give not your strength to loose women.' She can guide her son in any manner about any topic, but the first thing she decides to tell her son is not to become weak and vulnerable to promiscuous women. Just like us, this mother does not want her son, the king, to become involved with the wrong kind of woman. Notice, the rest of the verse says, '...nor your ways to those who and that destroy kings.' She is here letting her son know that there are people and things that will ruin him, and women, particularly promiscuous women, are a part of those who will destroy him." Grunts of agreement and understanding came from the women around the room.

"She then goes on for the next six verses to give him more advice about drinking and speaking up for the rights of others. Then she spends twenty-two verses telling her son about the kind of woman he should marry."

Lydia closed her bible and looked out at us. "I want you all to take some time right now to write a list of all the things about yourself that makes you a good woman, wife, and mother. Even if you do not have children or are not married, write down the qualities that you possess that would make you a good wife or mother. Be as detailed as possible. I will give you fifteen minutes of quiet time to create your lists."

For fifteen minutes, we worked on our lists, jotting down the traits that made us good women. I thought it would be easy to write my list; I knew I was a good woman, but for some reason I struggled with creating my list. I was smart, savvy, attractive, educated, spiritual, financially well off, and had a good sense of humor, but after writing down those things, I was stuck. I glanced around the room and noticed the other women also seemed to be thinking hard and slowly adding to their list. I refocused on my paper and pushed out several more attributes. I was giving, good with kids, kind (most of the time), a quick learner, ambitious, and supportive. Before I knew it, our fifteen minutes had ended, and Lydia was calling us back to attention.

"I am going to collect your lists and seal them in this envelope. During this course we are going to find out what Proverbs 31 says defines a virtuous woman. By the end of the course, we will have a clear definition of this woman, and then we will compare who you were coming into the class to the type of woman a queen would advise her son to marry." She walked around the room and gathered our lists while continuing to brief us about our next class. "During the week, please read, pray about, and mediate on verses ten and eleven. Make sure to bring your bibles and notebooks."

The class ended with a prayer, and we were dismissed. I left feeling a bit overwhelmed. The class had been interesting and compelling, causing me to want more immediately and not want to have to wait a whole week for the next lesson. As I approached my car to return home, my cell phone buzzed with an incoming call. I was still processing the class and not in the mood to deal with anyone, but I begrudgingly answered it.

"This is Amber Ross."

"Hi, Miss Ross. Samuel Perkins from Perkins, Gold & Associates. Sorry for calling you so late in the evening, but we just received word from Green Global Natural Foods Store that the executives are going to be in town tomorrow and want to set up a meeting with us about bringing the chain to Atlanta. Are you available to meet at 1 o'clock in the afternoon?"

I rolled my eyes and got into my truck. I didn't want to meet with them, especially at the last minute. These people acted as if I didn't have anything else to do; as if I waited around all day for them to call me. However, business was business so I gave in. "Hmm...I'll have to switch a few things around, but that's fine. Email me the information, and I'll see you tomorrow."

"Great! Thanks, Amber. We'll see you at one," he said before I impatiently hung up.

Slamming the door shut, I sighed heavily. "Great. Another meeting with the boys. The highlight of my week. I can't wait," I stated sarcastically before starting up my truck and heading home, tomorrow's meeting now on my mind and today's lesson in womanhood already forgotten.

Lesson 5: You Don't Have to Have the Last Word

A continual dripping on a day of violent showers and a contentious woman are alike;
Whoever attempts to restrain [a contentious woman] might as well try to stop the
wind–his right hand encounters oil [and she slips through his fingers]. (Proverbs
27:15-16)

As much as I enjoyed owning my own businesses, I hated dealing with men in
the workplace. Their misogynist attitudes got underneath my skin and often
caused me to act unreasonable. My Tuesday meeting was exactly as I feared it would
be; a bunch of well-to-do men overcompensating for their inadequacies, each one of
them trying to look like the big dog. Ugh!

Samuel Perkins and Jonathan Gold expected me to finance fifty percent of the
grocery store endeavor, but they refused to give me the respect and say of an equal
partner. Perkins, for the most part, was civilized, but his partner Gold was nothing
more than a sexist pig.

"What I am trying to say–," I began, but was cut short by Jonathan Gold.

"What Ms. Ross is trying to say is that although we are very much interested in
bringing this franchise to the Atlanta area, there are still some contractual issues that
need to be addressed." He looked at me and grinned, satisfied with his ability to
dominate the conversation.

"Ms. Ross can finish her sentences for herself, but thank you, Mr. Gold," I
passive-aggressively shot back at him and then continued to explain myself to the
Green Global executives. "We have outlined our concerns with the contract and
included them in the packet of information you have in front of you. We understand

that you will need time to look over our changes, consult with your attorneys, and get back to us."

Gold smirked, obviously offended by my comment. I didn't care. We had been playing this tit for tat game the entire meeting, and I refused to let him win. Perkins kept smiling nervously, afraid our behavior would negatively impact business. It wasn't the first time Gold and I power-struggled, but the boys knew they needed me and my resources, so Gold would have to continue to endure me.

After the meeting, Perkins pulled me to the side in the parking lot, confirming I was right about his nervous grin. "Amber, are you crazy?" he asked impatiently.

"No. Are you?" I asked slickly.

He sighed in irritation. "Look, I know my partner can be prideful at times, but insulting him repeatedly during a business meeting is immature and unproductive."

I unconsciously placed my left hand on my hip and rolled my neck. "Why are you having this conversation with me? Why aren't you telling him how immature he was acting? What? Because I am a woman I should have to bow down to him? I don't thinks so. This is my money too, and I will not be bullied or forced to take any foolishness from Gold, you, or anyone else." I starred him down, daring him to come at me again incorrectly.

"Ms. Ross, you are taking this thing out of proportion. I'll admit that Gold isn't a saint and can be a bit aggressive, but I need you to be the bigger person and handle things as a businesswoman, not feed into his behavior," he replied meekly attempting to defuse the tension.

I shook my head in disagreement. "Like I said before, why are you having this conversation with me? We haven't signed on any dotted lines so technically, I am not your partner; Gold, however, is. If you got a problem with the way things were handled today, you need to address them with him, and if you are no longer interested in doing business with me and my money, just say the word."

He rubbed his forehead in frustration. "Why do you have to take it there? Did I say anything about not wanting to do business with you? I am simply saying that you don't have to always have the last word."

"Well, I am not going to let him disrespect me. If that means having the last word, so be it," I replied unapologetically.

Samuel threw his hands up in the air in disbelief and resignation. "You know what? I give up. Let's just go our separate ways, cool off, and we will talk about this at another time."

I flashed a courteous smile. "Great. You have a nice day, Mr. Perkins."

I was fuming during my drive from the meeting to the real estate office. I didn't even call "my girl" Tisha because knowing her; she would have only pumped me up even more. By the time I walked into the front door, I was mentally daring someone to say something smart to me so I could completely go off. My office manager, a moderately attractive yet thrill-less guy named Eric Hayes, seemed to notice my brewing anger and attempted to play peacemaker.

"What's up, Boss? You seem edgy," he inquired as he walked into my office. The smell of his Burberry Cologne greeted me about the same time that he did. Although I had never considered dating anyone who worked for me, and Eric was definitely not my type, I had to admit that he always smelled wonderful.

I sighed heavily. "Do you really want to know?"

He took a seat in the faux-leather chair across from me. "I wouldn't have asked if I didn't."

I dropped a file that I had been thumbing through onto the table. "Men are my problem. Tell me something, Eric. Why can't men handle a successful woman? Why is it so difficult for you all to accept a woman who can hold her own? Are we really that intimidating?"

"Whoa! Intimidating? Are you serious?" he asked with raised eyebrows.

"Serious as trigonometry."

He leaned back in the chair, somewhat cocky in his demeanor. "I don't know too many men who are intimidated by a strong or successful woman. Leery maybe, but not intimidated."

"What?" I asked, but the word came out more like a statement. "So you mean to tell me that men don't feel threatened by women who are making more money or further advanced than they are?"

He shook his head in complete disagreement. "If a man feels threatened, it's not about the gender of the person, but how he perceives that person's assets will negatively impact his own."

"Then why do men treat me differently than they treat other men? Today, I was at this business meeting and one of the guys who wants me to partner with his company to start a new business kept challenging me, interrupting me, and treating me as if I wasn't capable of speaking for myself. He didn't act that way with anyone else except for me who was of course the only woman at the table. This isn't the first time with him or even with other men I've conducted business. It's always the same kind of rudeness and disrespect." I paused for a second as I thought about the day's events. The whole meeting flew through my mind in an instant, ending with my heated discussion with Mr. Perkins in the parking lot. "And what was even more annoying was that one of the partners actually said to me that I always have to have the last word. Am I supposed to sit back and let myself be treated like a doormat?"

Eric smiled as if he found what I was saying as humorous. "No, but truthfully, most men don't like argumentative women."

I gasped. "I am not trying to be argumentative; I just want to be treated fairly. They want my money and my help, but they can't treat me like an equal?"

"That's because in their eyes, it's not about you being an equal, it's about you being a woman," Eric stated without emotion. He had a way of being direct, straight to the point which was a quality I admired about him in relation to business, but while discussing my feelings, I was starting to hate his candidness.

I rolled my eyes. "See that's what I'm talking about!"

Sitting up in the chair, he pulled his body closer to my desk. "I'm going to say something, and I need you to listen and not jump down my throat. Can you do that?"

I sucked my teeth rebelliously. "Oh boy! Yeah, whatever. Say it."

He grinned at my childishness before speaking. "Okay, it's like this. Many men still hold onto traditional views of women, that women have a different role than men. Although society has changed, and men now have to work with women, they continue to hold on to the perspective that a man should be the leader."

I rolled my eyes again. "That is the most caveman-like philosophy I've ever heard. So, do you agree with them, that men should always be the leaders?"

"Well, to a certain extent. I work for you, so I have to respect you as my employer, but I am also a Christian, and my faith teaches me that a man is to be the head," he stated and leaned back in the chair again.

"But that is just in marriage," I countered.

"No, it's in everything. Honestly, how easy is it for a woman to run things all day long in her career and profession and then go home and humble herself to her husband? The marriage unit is the foundation of our world. How we deal with our significant others reflects how we deal with the world."

I sighed. "So what? Am I supposed to just give up my businesses so that men can feel as if they run the world?"

He shrugged his shoulders. "I can't tell you what you should do. And honestly, I need my job, so I wouldn't tell you to drop your businesses." He chuckled at his own self. "Giving up your business is not that deep, but it is something you are going to have to work out within yourself if you don't want to keep experiencing hostility from men or want to get married one day. Eventually, you are going to have to learn how to be a lady and a leader at the same time."

Eric's words echoed through my mind for the rest of the week. Over the course of two weeks, two very different men had suggested that I wasn't playing the role that a woman should play. I wanted to believe that both Chris and Eric were just idiots and bound by out-of-date gender stereotypes, but the truth was that Chris was getting married, and I was still very much single. I needed more from my life than a vibrant career, and to be honest, having money and status didn't make me happy. My house was quiet, my bed was lonely, and I found myself feeling envious of penniless housewives with four and five kids to feed on a warehouse employee's salary. My mind drifted back to the Wife 101 course. I had read the two verses as instructed by Lydia, but outside of what was obvious, I couldn't find any deeper meaning to the words or comfort for my situation. I found myself looking forward to the next class. Hopefully, the next lesson could shed some light on my increasingly disappointing relationships with men.

Lesson 6: Be a Jewel

A capable, intelligent, and virtuous woman – who is he who can find her? She is far more precious than jewels and her value is far above rubies or pearls. The heart of her husband trusts in her confidently and relies on and believes in her securely, so that he has no lack of [honest] gain or need of [dishonest] spoil. (Proverbs 31:10-11)

"This class we will focus on Proverbs 31:10-11. I hope you all did your homework, which was to read and meditate on these two verses. Just to be sure, I want everyone to take out their bibles and read the two verses again before we begin," Lydia Woods announced as the clock struck 7 p.m. on the following Monday night.

I took out my bible and read the verses as instructed. I had so many questions about this being a woman and wife thing, but I was too scared to ask them outright to Mrs. Woods. It was crazy that I dealt with business executives and people in high positions all the time, but for some strange reason, I was too timid to talk to a housewife-turned-relationship instructor. I went to class hoping and praying that we would naturally cover my questions during the lesson so that I wouldn't have to put myself in the spotlight.

After a couple minutes of silence, Lydia addressed the class again. "If you have been a Christian for some time, you have probably heard people teach, preach, or talk about being a virtuous woman. But what does it mean to be a virtuous woman? What defines a woman of virtue? Is it merely being a Christian woman or being good to others? Proverbs 31:10 asks us, who can find this woman? Now, we don't have to search high and low for the definition of a virtuous woman because after asking us such a question, our bible then explains the traits that make a woman virtuous." Lydia paused, scanned our faces, and then continued.

"Some of you may think that you are virtuous women already. I will not say that you aren't, but I am confident that by the time we go through these lessons and examine the many aspects of virtue, many of you who think you're virtuous will realize that you are not as virtuous as you thought you were. The question that is asked, 'Who can find...?' or in the Amplified version, 'Who is he who can find...?' suggests two things. One, something about men and the rarity of men who can successfully seek out and discover a virtuous woman and two, something about women, the rarity of women who actually are virtuous. I am sorry to burst some of your bubbles, but being virtuous is not common; it is rare. Think about it. The verse asks us 'who' as if this is something next to impossible. Of course, we know that finding a virtuous woman is not impossible, for God makes all things possible, but obviously this is not an easy or simple task for a man."

Lydia looked down at her bible. "The verse then goes on to further explain, 'She is far more precious than jewels and her value is far above rubies...' I know most of you know how precious and valuable jewelry can be." She looked up from her bible and smiled. "Jewelry is so precious and valuable that people take out insurance on it, hide it in safes, and put it underneath thick, protective glass. One of the things that always bothered me about this part of the verse is the idea of a virtuous woman being more valuable than rubies. I, like many of you, had been under the impression that diamonds were the most valuable jewel. Because of this shared view, I always wondered why the virtuous woman wasn't compared to diamonds. In my study time, the spirit led me to research rubies. What I learned was that certain rubies, large and transparent rubies, are rarer than diamonds and are more valuable than any other gem. Despite what is commonly known and thought about diamonds, there are rubies that are, in fact, more precious and valuable than diamonds. So when the verse compares the virtuous woman to a ruby, it is saying that she is the rarest and most valuable thing a man could have in his life. This verse also refers to pearls which most of us are aware are extremely valuable and interesting because they come forth from shells. The 'process' of a shell creating a pearl causes us to reflect on the development of something wonderful through an unsuspected means, like a butterfly coming from a caterpillar."

By this point, I was fascinated. I had read these scriptures on my own, but Lydia was making them come to life right before my very eyes. In amazement, I rested my elbow on the table in front of me and cradled my chin in the palm of my hand. I watched Lydia like a hawk as she paced the front of the classroom and continued the lesson.

"So why is this woman so special, so valuable, so highly regarded?" she hypothetically asked. "What does she bring to this man's life that makes her so necessary and rare? Verse eleven begins the description of who and what she is that causes her to be so significant."

Lydia laid her bible down on a desk and took a deep breath. "I am going to ask you all some questions, and I need you to raise your hand if the question applies to you. Now, I need you all to be completely honest. We cannot deal with our issues and get the help we need if we can't tell the truth. Okay?" Everyone in the class nodded in agreement.

"Show of hands, how many of you ladies work a job outside of your home?" Eight of the twelve women in the class, including me, raised our hands.

"Thank you." We lowered our hands. "How many work a job, but work from home?" One person's hand went up. Lydia smiled at her, and the lone woman put her hand back down.

"How many of you are housewives and do not hold a paying job?" The remaining three women raised their hands and then lowered them.

"How many of you who work feel you must work because of your family's financial obligations?" All nine of us who claimed to work either outside of the home or at home raised our hands.

"How many of you believe that if you did not work, your husband could be the sole provider for the family?" The three women who had acknowledged themselves as not working raised their hands along with two of the women who reported working outside the home.

"How many of you are concerned that if times got hard or if your husband was tempted that he would involve himself in wicked or illegal activities to gain money or possessions?" Half of the class raised their hands timidly and then dropped them.

Lydia smiled at the class and said, "Thank you all for your honesty."

She picked her bible back up from the table where it rested. "I grew up in a family with parents who were very supportive and dependable. Because they always took such good care of me, I never worried about my needs not being met. I trusted them to make sure that the family survived even the most difficult situations. When I went to school or lay down at night, I was free to focus on what I was doing and not anxious about what the family did or did not have. I never felt the need to steal, rob, or cheat because we were okay. If a wrong thought like stealing came to my mind, it wasn't due to our lack of money; it came from the sin and evil within me. Now, some people don't have my background and maybe some of you cannot relate to growing up in an environment of trust and faith in your parents, but if you did, you can begin to understand verse eleven."

Lydia's eyes scanned the opened book in her hand. "It reads, 'The heart of her husband trusts in her confidently and relies on and believes in her securely, so that he has no lack of honest gain or need of dishonest spoil.' What it is saying is that this woman is so trustworthy, so dependable, so reliable, so consistent, so faithful, so connected to God that her husband has everything he needs. This man doesn't have to worry about the family being okay; they already are. He is not plotting to do wrong acts to gain unnecessary possessions because he is content.

"Just like I knew as a child that I could rest in the care of my parents, this man can rest in the care of his wife. When he goes to work, he knows the money he makes will be spent well by her and used appropriately, whether he makes twenty thousand a year or two-hundred thousand a year. He is not sitting around anxious about whether or not the children are being taken care of or if there is food in the house or if his wife is cheating on him. He trusts her completely, and this high level of faith allows him to be a better, honest, peaceful, content man. He is not trying to keep up with the Joneses. He is satisfied and fulfilled because of his confidence in his wife.

"Wow! How many women do you know that have that type of impact on their husbands?"

The women in the class responded by shaking their heads and offering verbal grunts. I definitely did not have that kind of influence on a man. Truth be told, I couldn't even get a man to propose to me; much less trust me completely with his life. I listened attentively because I was dying to find out how to become a woman who was that powerful.

"Often as women, we fear that our spouses will not be able to provide for us or that they will go out and do wrong things to acquire more out of greed," she continued. "Verse eleven lets us know that if we are playing our role as a virtuous woman, these will not be issues. Our husbands will indeed be able to provide for the family, we will not experience lack, and he will not be tempted to gain unnecessary things by doing evil. Our husbands' behaviors are directly connected to ours as women. Who we are impacts who they are."

She shut her bible and looked out at us sternly. "If you want your husband to be a better man, you have to become a better woman. It is time to stop asking God to change him and time to start asking God to change you. This is why First Corinthians 7:14 states that the unbelieving husband is consecrated by his wife. As a married union, what we do as women is connected to what happens to our men. We have to stop playing the blame game, shooting our men down for their faults, and start asking ourselves, what do I need to do to become a better woman that will result in him becoming a better man?"

But I am a good woman, I thought. *What more do I have to do?* As much as I severely needed to know the answer to that question, I was also afraid of it. I had a feeling that the answer would rock my world and change life as I knew it. *Was I ready to change? Did I want marriage bad enough to change, especially if it meant sacrificing the things that I had come to hold dear?*

Lydia placed the bible back down and picked up her notepad. "For your homework, I want you to read and meditate on verses twelve and thirteen. I also want you to create a list. Write down all of the things that you have to do within a week to help keep your home and family in order.

"If you are not married, pretend that you are and list the things you would need to do if you had a husband. If you do not have children, pretend that you have at least one child and list all of the things you would need to do for a school aged child. This list should include household chores, childcare activities, and other wifely duties such as sex and communication with your husband. Do not include any activities that you do for your own career. Attached to each duty the average amount of time it takes you to do that activity each week. For example, it may take you six hours per week to wash everyone in your family's clothes, iron, fold, and put them away. If you have more children it may take longer. But write down an estimated time for each activity. Bring your lists with you to the next class."

Once again, class ended with prayer. I stuffed my bible and notebook in my bag and was headed out the door when Lydia stopped me. "Ms. Ross," she called out in a soft voice.

I stopped in my tracks and pivoted slowly to face her. The other participants quickly filed out of the room with the exception of a couple stragglers who remained in the rear of the room, socializing. "Yes?" I responded quizzically.

She approached me with a genuine grin. "I am glad to see that you have returned for the second lesson. How do you like the class so far?"

I wanted to scream out praises of adulation, but I instead settled for a meek, "I like it. I'm learning a lot."

"Wonderful. Are you keeping up? Do you have any questions? Are there any concerns or difficulties?" She spit questions at me like bullets from a loaded, machine gun.

I couldn't help but wonder why she seemed to be singling me out. There were others in the class, but somehow I only saw her doing the whole "one-on-one" thing with me. I wasn't the type to hold my tongue, and normally I would have confronted her about this by now, but there was something authentic about her that made me keep my blunt remarks to myself. "I am keeping up," I replied humbly.

"Well, if you have any questions, I mean anything thing at all, please call me. This is not a journey you have to take all by yourself."

I instantly wanted to cry. Alone, that was exactly how I felt. How did she know? There was so much that I wished I could share with her, but I wasn't ready to open up to a complete stranger. I was glad to know that if push came to shove, there was someone who would listen and who really cared.

"Thank you, Mrs. Woods," I responded gratefully before looking away. "I'll see you next week," I replied softly, and following her smile of understanding, I lowered my eyes and headed for the door.

Lesson 7: Never Underestimate the Little Guy

But the Lord said to Samuel, Look not on his appearance or at the height of his stature, for I have rejected him. For the Lord sees not as man sees; for man looks on the outward appearance, but the Lord looks on the heart.

(I Samuel 16:7)

When the unknown number showed up in the caller-ID of my cell phone, I should have seen it as a sign not to answer the call. However, being the inquisitive person that I am, I answered it–to my downfall.

"Ross, it's Gold."

I shut my eyes for a moment, trying to push away the negativity and muster up at least an ounce of kindness. Unfortunately for him, I couldn't find any. "And what did I do to deserve the honor of your phone call?" I asked with a hint of sarcasm.

"Ah, Ross! So typical. Nonetheless, Perkins asked me to relay a message. The Green Global Execs are throwing a party this weekend; actually, it's a dinner cruise. They want us and several other investors they are conducting business with in the South to be their special guests. Boarding starts at 6 p.m. and the boat leaves at 7 p.m. Friday night from Savannah. Can you make it?"

It was Tuesday. The event was less than three days away. I immediately felt aggravated. "Why is everything with them always so last minute?"

Gold chuckled. "I guess that's just how they do business. Anyway, it's a formal event, black tie, and so forth. Sounds like there will be about fifty or so people: politicians, movers and shakers, and whatnot. So put on a dress for once in your life and bring your man–well, you probably don't have a man, so bring one of your girlfriends and make sure she's cute. I might be able to squeeze her into my rolodex if she is hot enough."

I was livid. Put on a dress for once in my life? Bring a hot girlfriend? Moreover, how could he assume I didn't have a man? Well, I didn't, but I wasn't going to tell him that. He already thought he knew everything. "For your information, I wear plenty of dresses, I wouldn't bring my girlfriends anywhere near you, and I do have a man, not that he's any of your business."

Gold grunted in disbelief. "Yeah right, Ross. We'll see on Friday. I look forward to seeing you in your dress and with this man, on the boat. I'll email you the invite."

"Fine." I hung up the phone proudly. Then it hit me. What did I just do? The dress part was easy, but I didn't have a man to take with me to the dinner! There was no way that I could face Gold dateless. What was I going to do? Call Tisha? No! She'd only try to hook me up with Rude Boy again. "Who can I...Eric!" I rushed out of my office and down the hall toward his.

"Eric, I need your help!" I yelled as I pushed open the door and ran toward his desk.

He looked up from his computer. "What's up, Boss?"

"Are you busy Friday night?"

He smiled coyly. "Are you asking me on a date...or to work late?"

"A little bit of both." I started to pace back and forth in front of his desk and ramble. "I have to go to this dinner cruise in Savannah, and I need a date. I sort of told this arrogant associate of mine that I had a man, which I don't, at least not anymore. I can't show up alone because he will, he will...Please don't make me go alone! I will comp your time, pay you overtime, anything you want, just say yes...please!" I slammed my hands on top of his desk; my palms hit the wood causing a loud thud.

He sat back in his chair and smirked. "I don't think I've ever seen you beg. It's kind of flattering."

"Eric!"

"Okay, okay, I'll go. Give me Monday off and we should be even."

I exhaled in relief. "Terrific. It's a black tie function, but don't worry. If you write down your measurements, I can have a tuxedo sent to you."

"I get a tux? This is getting better and better," he said as he pulled out a sticky note, wrote down his measurements, and handed the paper to me.

Exhausted, I plopped down into the empty chair in front of him. "It is in Savannah so we will take the day off on Friday and drive down there. The cruise probably won't make it back to land before 9 p.m. so I'll book us a couple of hotel rooms, and we can drive back Saturday morning. I think that covers the details. Thanks so much for doing this, Eric. You're a lifesaver!"

"Hey, I'm getting a free tux, a dinner cruise, hotel room, trip to Savannah, a Friday away from the office, and Monday off, and all I have to do is pretend I have a rich girlfriend. This is my come up! What are you getting out of all of this?"

"Ha ha ha, funny. I get to hold on to a piece of my dignity, and correction, I'm not rich; I'm financially secure."

"Give me a raise, and I'll call you whatever you want me to call you," he joked.

I stood up and laughed. "It's time for you to get back to work!"

He pouted. "See, you do people favors and this is how they treat you."

The rest of the week moved along uneventfully. I had a tuxedo sent to Eric's house the next day, booked two suites at the in Marriott downtown Savannah, and even hit up Macy's for a new dress. I called the managers at Sweet Tooth Oasis and Sunrise Sunset to let them know I would be out of town on Friday and Saturday. I even had dinner with Tisha on Thursday night at a trendy new restaurant called Sublime to catch up with the who, what, when, where, and whys of our lives. By the time I pulled up to Eric's apartment at noon on Friday in my royal blue Mustang, I was ready for a nice evening on the water and to curl up in a king size bed at the hotel, maybe even order room service.

Knowing that I don't like waiting on people, Eric was waiting for me at the curb in front of his Lawrenceville apartment. I stopped the car in front of him, turned off the engine, and popped the trunk. He threw his duffle bag into the trunk and hopped in the passenger seat, gazing around the vehicle in delight.

"Sweet! I didn't know you had a muscle car. Love the color! I'm going to start calling you, Mustang Sally."

"Ride, Sally, ride," I sang.

Eric started snapping his fingers and joined in. "Mustang Sally. Guess you better slow your Mustang down."

"Slow it down, slow it down," I sang in a low voice.

We both looked at each other and burst into laughter at our horrible singing. Once we controlled our laughter, I started the car back up, and we headed down I-75 towards Macon, Georgia. The ride to Macon went quickly. We filled the time with discussion about cars: those we've had and those we still were waiting to get. From there, the conversation naturally changed into crazy car stories about things that have happened to us and friends while in our automobiles. By the time we stopped in Macon for food and to get gas, my stomach was hurting and I was crying from laughing at Eric's ridiculous stories.

"For real! I'm on the side of the road with a bicycle pump, trying to pump up the flat. I was working hard too. Sweating and everything!" Eric said in between laughs.

I wiped the tears from my eyes. "You're a fool! Oh my! I haven't laughed that hard in years. I can hardly breathe."

I caught my breath while Eric filled up my car with unleaded gasoline. Noticing a Subway sandwich store in the same plaza as the gas station, I walked over to it and purchased us a couple of 6-inch turkey subs, bags of chips, and iced teas.

Back on the road, we turned up the stereo, listened to the newest Kirk Franklin CD, and ate our late lunch as we cruised 75 mph down I-16 East toward Savannah.

We arrived in Savannah around 4 p.m. and immediately checked into the hotel, showered, and changed. By 6:30, we were on the dinner boat, looking fabulous like we had just stepped off the pages of *People* Magazine. Eric cleaned up well, I had to admit. The ebony colored tux with an olive green and silver vest suited his mocha complexion, bringing out his regal African features. I admired him closely, proud of myself for turning another "maybe" into a "positively yes!"

Noticing my approval, Eric morphed into player mode and smoothly moved toward me with a classic line. "I'm sorry, but I don't think I've had the pleasure of meeting the most beautiful woman on this boat. My name's Eric Hayes, and you are?"

"Out of your league, Playboy!"

We laughed discreetly, trying not to gain the attention of those around us. The energy in the air was stifling. Wannabes mingled with people with too much money and not enough fervor in hopes of sucking them dry. I hadn't yet seen Gold, but I was sure he would emerge sooner or later and I was ready for round #9. I was wearing an olive green, satin, halter top dress that flowed elegantly to the floor. A small, silver cashmere jacket covered my bare shoulders and arms, helping me to stay warm against the cool February air. Pearls, which were my favorite jewelry hung from my ears, neck, and wrist. After being at the last Wife 101 class, pearls now held an even greater sentiment for me.

As I reached upwards to make sure no strands of my hair had gone rogue, the monstrous laugh of Gold sliced through my glee, sending a wave of fear down my spine. Could I really pull this off? The moment of truth.

I elbowed Eric and nodded in the direction of Gold, informing him that it was time to get to work. Catching my drift, Eric stepped closer to me and wrapped his arm around my waist, sealing our relationship with a kiss on the forehead as Gold approached.

Gold stopped short in front of us, chuckling before tipping his wine glass towards me. "Ross! Wow! I guess I was wrong. You really do own a dress…and a man too. How about that?"

"Yeah, Gold, but I was right. You really are a jerk."

Eric, feeling the tension mounting between Gold and me, intervened. "Hi, how are you. I'm Eric Hayes." The men shook hands.

"Jonathan Gold. Ms. Ross and I, along with my associate Samuel Perkins, are considering partnership, but you should already know that." He smiled cynically.

Eric jumped into action, unaffected by Gold's mocking tone. "Yes. The Green Global Natural Food Store. It would be a great addition to the Metro Atlanta area. We only have a few whole foods grocery stores and with the increasing demand for healthier lifestyles, it would be a perfect time to get into the market."

Gold's smile turned uncertain, but I could tell he still wasn't fully convinced. "Our sentiments exactly…I can't help but wonder how did you two lovebirds meet?"

"Uh, well we–," I began, but was rescued by Eric.

"Ironically, we also are business associates. We met through a real estate opportunity a few years back. Amber has been a special part of my life ever since." Eric pulled me closer and looked into my eyes, showering me with unnerving attention. He was really good; I had to give him credit.

Gold, realizing he was down for the count, gave up. "I see. Well I don't want to monopolize all of your time, and it seems the boat is leaving the port. It's nice to meet you, Mr. Hayes. Ross, enjoy your evening."

As Gold walked away, I could have sworn I heard bells ringing and the announcer saying, "And the winner is by TKO…Amber Ross!" I was elated. I would seriously have to consider giving Eric that raise.

"Thank you! You were amazing!" I complimented Eric as soon as Gold was out of sight.

"We aim to please. Now, Ms. Ross, you should exhale and enjoy some of these shrimp cocktails because I know I am about to!" Eric's comedic timing was impeccable.

A few hours later, we parted ways as we headed to our separate hotel suites for the night. I was stunned by the wonderful time I had with Eric. Who knew he was such a blast to be around? Our past interactions were strictly within the office and business related. It never occurred to me that he could end up being someone I could hang out with outside of work. Honestly, I had invited him to Savannah only because I was desperate, he was available, and since he worked for me I knew he wouldn't say no.

The more I thought about him, Eric was actually a pretty good catch. He was handsome, humorous, and genuine, and he had a good work ethic. I didn't know too much about him (which was my fault), but I was pretty certain that he was single. That had to be a telltale sign. Why would a great man be single in a city where women outnumbered men 12-to-1? Something was definitely wrong with him. Maybe he was one of those down low brothers. I wouldn't put it past him or any man. We lived in Atlanta, Georgia, the Mecca of black homosexuality.

I dove into the bed and snuggled deep under the thick, mustard colored comforter and soft, white cotton sheets. "Umm," a satisfactory groan escaped my lips. As much as I was in heaven at that moment, nestled in award-winning hospitality, I found myself wondering what Eric was doing a few doors over. Was he asleep already or catching up on sports TV like a typical man? Was he enjoying a hot shower or calling his secret lover back home? I laughed at myself for my outrageous imagination and turned over in the bed. It was definitely time to go to sleep before I ended up in front of Eric's room with my ear pressed against the door, trying to ease drop on his personal life.

The ride back to Atlanta was quiet. We left early, around 8 a.m., stopping in Dublin, Georgia, at a Waffle House for breakfast. We both must have had other things consuming our thoughts because even while sipping on coffee and munching on cheese grits, bacon, eggs, and waffles, we had very little to say. A few times, I noticed Eric gazing out the window, his eyes glossed over, but I just chalked up his daze and silence to fatigue. I was glad I'd given him Monday off of work so that he could re-energize. His day off also meant I would have to cover his duties for the day.

When I dropped him off at his apartment, he still seemed preoccupied. "Thanks for the trip," he said as he leaned into the car after retrieving his duffle bag from the trunk. "I really enjoyed everything. Please let me know if you ever need an escort again. I'd be happy to oblige."

"No, thank you! You really helped me big time. Enjoy your Monday off," I replied before smiling, waving goodbye, and pulling away from the curb.

My entire drive home I fought with the pestering thought that Eric was one of the good ones. As much as I wanted to remain in denial, he was the kind of man a woman could get used to quickly. Thank goodness that he was my employee, and I had a strict no fraternizing rule. Good guy or not, Eric was off limits.

Lesson 8: Maintain a Drama-Free Zone

She comforts, encourages, and does him only good as long as there is life within her.

She seeks out wool and flax and works with willing hands [to develop it].

(Proverbs 31:12-13)

"Last week I told you all to create a list of the various activities that you need to do in order to take care of your home and family," Lydia said at the start of our next Wife 101 class.

"I also asked you to estimate how much time it takes you to do each task on a weekly basis and to include the time on your list. Now, there are 168 hours in a week. Twenty four hours times 7 days in a week, gives you 168 hours. Each of us should be getting 8 hours of sleep per day. I know some of you get less or more, but for the sake of this activity, we are going to say everyone is sleeping 8 hours per day, times 7 days a week, giving us 56 hours of sleep time per week. If we subtract our sleep hours from our total hours, we are left with 112 hours a week to do all of the things that we need to do.

"Now, let's say we all work full-time jobs, and we only work 40 hours per week, no overtime. Let's also say that it takes us 30 minutes to get to work each day and 30 minutes to get home each day, so out total time spent working outside the home is 45 hours per week if we work 5 days per week." She looked around the room, searching for glazed over eyes. "Are you all following me?"

We nodded even though we were still wondering where she was going with all of her calculations, or at least I was.

"So, 112 hours were left after we've deducted our sleep time, and now deducting 45 hours for working outside the home, we are now left with 67 hours per week to take care of everything else in our lives. If we divided 67 hours by 7 days a week, we basically have about 9.5 hours per day to do everything from bathing, grooming, eating, cooking, cleaning, taking care of children, shopping, quality time with spouse, attending social activities, having down time, etc.

"If you are a working wife and mother you have less than 10 hours per day to do all that you need to do. Alternatively, if you are a wife or mother who does not work a job, you have 16 hours per day to do all that you need to do.

"The big question is how much time do you really need each day to get everything done? Please take out your lists and add up all of the time you have on your list connected to your wifely and motherly activities." Once we all had out lists out and in front of us, she asked, "Can I get a volunteer to read their list to the class?"

A full figured woman with a medium brown complexion and a short cropped hairdo raised her hand to volunteer. After being recognized by Lydia, she walked up to the front of the class with her notebook in her hand.

"My name is Sarah, and I am married and have an 8 year old son. Uh, I spend about 13 hours a week bathing and grooming my son, 15 hours cooking, 14 hours cleaning, 7 hours doing laundry, 6 hours shopping for food, clothing, and other household needs, 2 hours for sexual intimacy, 10 hours a week having one-on-one time with my husband, 6 hours going over homework or doing educational activities with my son, 12 hours grooming myself, 5 hours doing social activities like church or attending gatherings, 2 hours paying bills, and 10 hours taking my son to his activities or having family time. Altogether, it is 76 hours a week which, wow, is a lot of time."

Lydia placed her index finger and thumb on her chin as if she were thinking. "It is. Let me ask you another question, Sarah. Do you work and if so, how many hours per week?"

"Yes, I work fulltime, at least 40 hours a week."

"So how is this possible when if you followed our original model you only have 67 hours when you work fulltime, and you just said you are spending 76 hours a week taking care of your family. This means there are 9 hours per week that you don't have, but you need. Also you have not factored in alone time with God or down time for yourself. How much time per week do you spend alone with God? And how much time per week do you do things for yourself like reading, watching TV or a movie, talking on the phone, or other stuff like that?"

Sarah shook her head, seeming baffled by the truth. "Honestly, I don't get a lot of time to do any one of those things, but I would say I like to spend 30 minutes in the morning and at night praying or reading my word, so it would be like 7 hours a week for alone time with God. I probably get maybe 1-2 hours a day to myself so maybe 14 hours a week for down time."

Lydia picked up a calculator from the table up front and loaded several numbers into it. "So now you are 30 hours in the hole. Where are these 30 hours coming from? You only get 168 hours per week, so where are you taking these extra 30 hours from?"

A look of guilt washed over Sarah's face. "Sad to say, but I don't usually get 8 hours of sleep per night. I may get 5 or 6 at the most. I probably don't spend as much time as I need to with God or my husband. I don't know. I am always busy."

"My point exactly! We are always busy, and we don't get to spend the time we need to on important stuff because we don't have the time. Especially if we work traditional jobs, we really don't have the time. If Sarah did not work, she would have enough time to do everything on her list including sleep, and she would still have 10 hours a week left over to use as she wishes. I am not trying to convince you all not to work, but I am just demonstrating how stretched we are as women."

The room was quiet. Although no one else read her list, we all knew the result would be similar. For me, owning three businesses, my hours spent working were astronomical. To top it all off, I was considering partnership for a fourth business. Did a husband and children fit into my lifestyle at all? Was I really willing to give up all that I had worked so hard to build for a family? Did God want me to give it all up? If so, why did he give it to me in the first place? I couldn't help but feel a little depressed by the thought of letting go of my current lifestyle.

Lydia put down the calculator and picked up her bible. "As we continue through this class, other duties may come up and you can add them to your list accordingly. We will discuss the list again in two weeks, but until then, you may put them away."

"We have spent a lot of time on our lists, but I still want to go over our verses for the week which are Proverbs 31:12-13. Let's read them quietly."

"Verse 12 states, 'She comforts, encourages, and does him only good as long as there is life within her.' If you considered this passage in reverse, it would say she never makes him uncomfortable, discourages, or does him wrongly as long as she is living. Okay honestly, what woman has ever met this standard? Who can really say that they have always encouraged their man, always have comforted him, and never done him wrong? Even us good Christian women 'cut a fool' sometimes, especially when they have gotten on our nerves or have mistreated us. Am I right?"

"Right," was heard from various women in the group.

"But this virtuous woman is a drama free woman. When that man comes home in a foul mood, complaining about his job, she says, 'Baby it's gonna be okay. God is with you.' When he gets laid off and can't find work for six months she says, 'God will provide, just keep the faith.' When she finds out that he has gambled their bill money away, does she curse him out and leave with the kids? No. She tells him, 'I'm praying for you, that God will help you make good decisions that will help our family and not hurt it.' How many of you could do that all the time?"

The room was quiet. I was thinking to myself, *Not me! I wish a man would gamble our bill money away! We would have to fight straight-up!*

Lydia continued, "Once again, the point of this is not to make you feel that you are a bad woman, but to show you how you can be a better woman. If we want better men, we must become better women.

"Verse 13 says, 'She seeks out wool and flax and works with willing hands to develop it.' Now, here is where I am going to confuse you. From verse 13 on we begin to hear a lot about how hard this woman works. We started today's class talking about how your time is limited, especially if you work, and how much more time you would have if you didn't carry a job. However, the virtuous woman is not your typical housewife. She just doesn't cook and clean and watch the children. No, that's not her."

Lydia smiled, knowing she had us right where she wanted us, begging for more information. "She knows how to make things, she knows how to run a business, she knows how to buy things and get the most for her money. She is creative and innovative. She works very hard. She is the epitome of good work ethic."

Lydia looked around the room and shook her head. "I know what you all are thinking: Am I supposed to work or not? Here is the truth; the problem with today's woman is that we get caught up in man's work system instead of God's. We get jobs like we are men, for the sole purpose of a paycheck as if we are expected to be the breadwinner. Half the time we hate what we do, but we do it anyway. We are losing out on quality time with our family for a job that often doesn't pay enough and that we aren't even committed to in our hearts. What's up with that? We are completely missing the point."

She flipped the pages of her bible. "The bible tells us in Colossians 3:23, 'Whatever may be your task, work at it heartily, from the soul, as something done for the Lord and not for men.' If we are going to give up so much of ourselves to a job, it should be something we do for God, not man. And this is not about working for a church's ministry! Working in the church is good and fine, but as we continue to learn about this virtuous woman, she works from the heart and soul, but does not take place within the walls of the church.

"Listen, I'm not knocking anyone's job or what you feel you need to do to keep your family afloat, but life with God is all about faith, and faith without works is dead. I work now, and I make good money, but what I do professionally no longer competes with my home life. I don't have to choose between being a good mother and being a good worker. That was never God's plan for us. When you start feeling like you have to choose between being there for your family and getting a paycheck, you're heading down the wrong road. Your faith is rooted in your job and not in God." Looking exasperated, Lydia put down her bible.

"I know we've talked about a lot tonight; some things that may cause inner conflict. When we're apart, please pray over these things and ask God to reveal His truth to you about these matters; don't just take my word for it. The bible tells us to ask for understanding because God gives it freely. For next week, study verses fourteen and fifteen."

Riding home from the class, I felt overwhelmed by the lesson. A million questions seemed to consume my brain, causing an instant headache. Was I working for God or man? Did I see my work as a paycheck or something more? Were my heart and soul in the equation? Did I trust God? Was my faith dead? Was God proud of me for my work or was I completely missing the point? Moreover, was my work interfering with my ability to be a good candidate for marriage and children?

I was so perplexed. I wanted to stay after class and ask Lydia more questions, but I was too afraid of the answers I might receive. I left, feeling more unsure about myself than when I started the class. A part of me wanted to give up, let this wife class go and just accept a life without marriage, but something, a little small voice, prodded me to see it through to the end. Despite my ongoing frustration and bewilderment, I planned to return the next week. The way I saw it, I had nothing to lose (except a little bit of my sanity), and the possibility of the life that I really wanted to gain.

Lesson 9: Appreciate the Little Things

Better is little with the reverent, worshipful fear of the Lord than great and rich treasure and trouble with it. (Proverbs 15:16)

There is one day a year that every single woman dreads (better yet, some married women hate it too), Valentine's Day. Who was the genius who started this foolishness? Is it a conspiracy to make unattached people feel worse than they already do? If so, it's working.

I despised Valentine's Day so much that I had devised a plan on how to get through the day without having an emotional breakdown. Step 1: Bury myself in work. I stayed chained to my desk at the real estate office. I avoided the pastry shop (Valentine's Day was our busiest holiday for obvious reasons), as well as the daycare (for some weird reason parents always seemed to send their children to daycare with Valentine's goodies). However, no one in the free world seemed to care about real estate on Valentine's Day, which was fine by me. Step 2: Stay far away from stores. Every store from the local gas station to Wal-Mart was evil on Valentine's Day. Every merchant realized that adding a few heart shaped chocolates, long stemmed roses, and stuffed teddy bears to the inventory would prove to be lucrative. Step 3: Eat in. Although I didn't cook much, Valentine's Day was a good day to make use of my expensive cookware. Going to any restaurant with the exception of fast food spots was like begging to get my feelings hurt. Step 4: Avoid all technology. Why do people think that picture messaging you a rose or sending you a text that reads "HAPPY VALENTINE'S DAY" is cute? Don't post any hearts on my Facebook wall, don't forward me any adorable Valentine's emails, and definitely don't call me wishing me a happy day! On Valentine's Day my cell phone was muted. I checked my voicemails periodically, but my texting feature was turned off. I screened and deleted unwanted emails, and I refused to login to any social media sites. Like I said, I had a plan.

I would have stuck firmly to my plan had Eric not walked into the office at 9 a.m. carrying a dozen yellow roses and a heart shaped cookie cake from Sweet Tooth Oasis! The nerve of him! I was about to chew him out for using my own bakery to annoy me when he suavely placed the roses and cake on my desk and said, "Good Morning, Boss. Happy Valentine's Day. I know you don't have a man in your life, so I figured I would have to be the one to make your day special."

I almost melted. I had never witnessed anything so thoughtful and especially done for me. Okay, my mind was made up; I would most certainly have to give him a raise. "Eric, this is the sweetest thing anyone…Wow! Thank you…You know, if you're trying to earn that raise, it's looking really promising for you."

He pumped his fist in the air and did the cabbage patch dance. "Yes!"

I chuckled. "Oh, so this was all for a raise, huh?"

"Come on, Boss. If this was for a raise, I would have already spent my few extra pennies on these flowers and this cake. Do you know how expensive roses are on V-Day? And you are making a killing at Sweet Tooth Oasis! That place was packed!"

I picked up the roses and smelled them. Their smell was intoxicating. "I know. I always have to put extra people on the schedule during this time of year to handle the crowd. Valentine's Day, Mother's Day, Graduation, and Christmas are our peak holidays."

He smiled and shook his head. "Do you know that you are living every man's dream?"

"What?" I sniffed the flowers again.

He leaned against my desk. "No matter what a man tells you, every man wants to be successful. Own his-own business, call the shots, and make lots of money in the process. You are doing that now, and you're still young. You own three businesses, and I'm pretty sure, especially since you have a real estate company, that you have more than one residential property in your name. I mean really, you own the buildings your businesses occupy! It must be nice."

I disliked people making that comment to me, like my life was so perfect. Well it wasn't. "Sometimes, it isn't all it's cracked up to be. I love seeing my goals come to life, but it's like it's never enough. No matter how much I gain, I'm never satisfied. There's always something missing."

"Well, I'm going to say this. I can see why you're still single. You are an awesome woman, but most men are still trying to get to where you're at. It's hard for us to be out here trying to make things happen and then date a woman who has everything we want. It's a major blow to our self-esteem as men. Often we feel like we have nothing to offer you. Like why would you want to be with someone who can't do more for you than you can do for yourself? Men like to feel needed, but you seem as if you don't need anyone or anything."

I sucked my teeth. "That is so not fair. I have needs. They may not be as typical as needing a man to provide financially for me, but I still have needs."

"Yeah, I know you do, but it takes a really patient and understanding man to get to know you well enough to figure out what those needs are." He sighed and looked at me sympathetically. "Listen, why don't you allow me to treat you to dinner this evening? Please don't say you have a date because I know you'd be lying."

I couldn't let him do so much. I paid him fairly, but I made way more money than him. It wasn't right for me to let him cover the bill. "You've already done enough for me today; let me at least pay for dinner."

"Boss, I mean, Amber. Let me be the man. I can afford dinner. I was only talking about McDonald's."

We laughed.

"No seriously, Amber. I'll take you to a fairly decent restaurant. You pay me enough to do that."

I thought about Chris' comment that I didn't let men be men. Maybe he had a point. Maybe I just didn't know how to let a man take care of me. I was so used to taking care of myself and everyone else for that matter. Possibly I had to be more open about my needs, as Eric was suggesting. I took a deep breath and smiled authentically. "Okay. Dinner is on you."

To make the evening more exciting and less awkward, I invited Tisha and her new beau Kevin to join us for dinner, of course with Eric's approval. We decided to go to *Arizona's*, an American cuisine restaurant in Lithonia, near Stonecrest Mall. Eric knew the manager and got us bumped to the front of the waiting list and prime seating near the fireplace, across from where the live jazz band was setup and playing. The ambiance was so romantic that I secretly wished I was on a date with the man I loved versus on a pity dinner with my employee and best friend.

Our food arrived as the band began playing an old, Jill Scott tune. The big afro wearing vocalist belted out the lyrics of "He Loves Me" as if her life depended on it.

You love me

Especially

Different...

I felt myself get sucked into a trance, falling deeply into the lull of the enchanting live music. By the time I came back to earth, my lamb ribs were cold.

Finished eating, Trish the multi tasker was pushing Kevin away as he attempted to nibble on her neck and grilling Eric, simultaneously. "So Eric, you're not married or dating anyone?"

"No."

"Are you gay?"

"No."

Kevin moved in again for a kiss, but Tisha pushed him away, glaring at him in the process. She cut her eyes at him and then turned her attention back to Eric. "Do you have children?"

"Yes, I have a daughter. Jonelle."

"Really? How old?"

"She's nine."

"Do you pay your child support?"

"Yes."

"On time?"

"I've been late a few times when I've been out of work, but I always take care of my child. She has never gone without."

"Why didn't you marry your child's mother? Did she catch you cheating?"

Eric smirked. "No. She wasn't happy, and in the process she made my life miserable."

"Why? Weren't you enough man for her?"

"You'll have to ask her about that."

Tisha gave him an unconvinced look. "You honestly don't know?"

Eric shrugged. "We just weren't right for each other."

Tisha stared him down. "So you never cheated?"

Eric sat back in his seat, something I noticed that he did when he wanted to let others know that they weren't getting to him. "Did I cheat on her? No. Have I ever cheated on a woman? Yes; I'm not perfect. I've made my fair share of mistakes in relationships, but I'd like to believe that I am older and wiser now. I take commitment more seriously now than I used to."

Tisha grinned. I knew she was enjoying playing the investigative role and would not stop asking questions until all of Eric's business was laid out on the table. "When was the last time you dated someone?"

"About six months ago or so."

"What happened?"

"I didn't see her as the type of woman I could be with long term. Anymore questions?" Eric challenged.

"Yep. Are you interested in my best friend?"

"What?" Eric and I both asked at the same time.

Tisha leaned in closer to ensure he heard her. "Are you trying to get with Amber? Do you like her?"

I jumped to his defense. "Eric, you do not have to answer that question. Tisha, why are you bothering him?"

"He asked me if I had any more questions, and I did. What's the deal with y'all anyway?"

"There is no deal. Eric is one of my most valued employees who has become somewhat of a friend. He has graciously invited me to dinner knowing that I didn't have a date tonight. Give him a break; he's a good guy."

"So if he is such a good guy, why aren't you two hooking up? I'm just trying to get the 4-1-1. What's up?"

"What's up is the check. We need to pay it and roll out because it must be past your bedtime. You're starting to sound crazy. Where's that waitress?" I scanned the restaurant for our server and upon making eye contact with her, mouthed the word "check" so she would hurry up and bring it before Tisha embarrassed me any further. Uncomfortably, I looked over at Eric and gave him a half smile. He chuckled, shook his head in amusement, and reached for his wallet.

After dinner, Eric drove me back to the office to pick up my truck.

"Thanks for the ride and dinner and the flowers and the cake and just everything. You turned a bad day into a good one," I said to Eric as I grabbed my purse, unsnapped the seat belt, and pulled on the passenger side door handle to exit his older, but well cared for, Chevy Impala.

I was halfway out the door when I felt Eric's hand around my left wrist. I quickly turned my head back and frowned at him, causing him to release me. He grinned and replied, "You know, I could have answered Tisha's question back at the restaurant."

"Huh?"

"When Tisha asked me if I liked you. I could have answered her. You didn't have to intervene."

I let out a nervous giggle. "Oh. Tisha is just…Tisha. I'm sorry about all that."

Eric's eyes roamed from my face down to my hands and back up to my face again. "Don't be. The truth is that I do like you."

His words hit me like bricks. I blinked a few times at their impact. "What? Come again?"

"I said that I like you. I never really thought about it until we did the whole dinner cruise thing in Savannah. I was actually surprised by how much I enjoyed being with you. Up until then everything has been purely professional, but lately I've gotten to see a different side of you, a side that is very alluring."

"You're serious?"

He rubbed his hands together. "Yeah. But hey, I know that you are my boss, and I'm not trying to make this weird for you. So if you're not interested, simply say so now, and I promise to respect that, and we can pretend like this never happened."

"Wow!" The roomy car began to feel crowded and stuffy. I wasn't claustrophobic, but for some reason I felt like my throat was closing up, and I couldn't breathe. I tightened the grip on my purse. "I…don't know what to say. I've enjoyed hanging out with you too, but I don't know if…Would it be okay if I thought about it for a few days?"

"Sure. Take all the time you need. No pressure." He gave me a sincere smile.

I quickly looked away. "Thanks. And thanks again for a wonderful evening." I needed air and immediately rushed out of his car into the brisk night air. I wanted to fall apart right then, but I knew he was watching me, so I opted to play it cool while I walked to my truck, got in, and started the engine. Once I pulled away from the building, he drove in a different direction, and I instantly unraveled.

Hot tears plummeted down my face, and the bizarre part was that I didn't know why. A man told me that he was interested in me, and my response was to cry? Seriously, Amber? Deep down I had to admit to myself that I was afraid. I had been hurt so many times, and after the whole Chris catastrophe, I wasn't sure that I could handle putting my heart on the line again. Yes, I did like Eric, honestly, I liked him a lot, but dating him could ruin our work relationship, and worse, I could end up with a broken heart.

I drove home in a funk, allowing tears to fall over every man who had ever let me down. Ethan, Gerald, Sammy, Isaac, Reggie, David, Carlos, and Chris; each story different yet the same. I couldn't help but wonder if saying yes to Eric would add him to the list of disappointed exes. By the time I pulled into my garage, I was still utterly confused, so I resolved to handle the situation the only way I knew how: I prayed for God's direction.

Lesson 10: Work the Night Shift

She is like the merchant ships loaded with foodstuffs; she brings her household's food from a far [country]. She rises while it is yet night and gets [spiritual] food for her household and assigns her maids their tasks. (Proverbs 31:14-15)

"How many of you still live in the city where you were raised?" Lydia's eyes roamed the room as a few hands shot up. Most of the class being migrants to Atlanta kept our hands down and waited for Lydia to make her point.

"In today's society, we often move to a different city, state, or sometimes country after getting married," Lydia continued. "Most times it is because of a job opportunity, but not always. A family might relocate because of weather conditions, educational opportunities, distance from relatives, financial benefits, or simply comfort.

"In biblical times, a woman was given by her family to her husband when she married. Wherever he lived or planned to go, it was expected that she follow him. It was not uncommon for a new wife to have to move instantly to another village, city, or country to start her new life with her husband, sometimes never seeing her family again."

Lydia picked up her bible and flipped it open to the page marked off by a thin piece of red ribbon. Now familiar with her teaching style, many of us took out our bibles and turned to the book of Proverbs.

"Proverbs 31:14 states, 'She is like the merchant ships loaded with foodstuff; she brings her household food from a far country.' This virtuous wife is not coming into the marriage or her family empty handed with nothing to offer. She is someone who has gained a lot and learned a lot from her own family and background and is now bringing all of it to her husband and children.

"The verse mentions food, but food is not just what you eat physically' it is everything that nourishes you. You can have mental food, spiritual food, emotional food, and so on. So when the verse talks about her being loaded with food and bringing food, it doesn't have to pertain to edible items. Yes, she could bring with her some family recipes and even some special foods or spices from her homeland, but she can also bring wisdom from her ancestors, knowledge from her teachers, lessons from her advisors."

Lydia walked back and forth across the front of the room while continuing her lesson. "I often hear people ask, 'What are you bringing to the table?' When they ask this question they are talking about evaluating a person's compatibility in a relationship based on what they have to offer the other person or visa-versa. The virtuous wife is coming to the table with overflowing arms. She brings with her a wealth of intangible assets from her homeland, from her people, and from her God.

"What are you bringing to the table? Is it a bunch of typical possessions: a house, car, bank account, etc? Or do you have more to offer? See, eventually the money will run out, the house can fall apart, or the car might breakdown, but traits like wisdom, kindness, honesty, gentleness, understanding, faith, passion, compassion, and authenticity never get lost in the shuffle. You can always pull from them for nourishment."

What Lydia said caused me to question myself. What was I bringing to the table? I had always assumed that I had a lot to offer because of my career success, but now that the focus was on godly traits, I felt as if my stock, like the Dow Jones, was plummeting. Maybe I wasn't as great of a catch as I believed I was. Eric liked me, but then again Eric really didn't know me well. Possibly once we got to know each other better, he would also run like Chris had.

"One final thought about verse fourteen," Lydia said. "Importing goods has always been a lucrative business. Often certain items need to be imported because certain foreign counties specialize or are abundant in demanded products. When the verse compares the virtuous woman to merchant ships from a far country, it also hints at this woman being valuable, in demand, highly needed, and someone worth waiting for."

Lydia smiled then glanced downwards and pulled her bible closer to her face. "Verse fifteen reads, 'She rises while it is yet night and gets spiritual food for her household and assigns her maids their tasks.' If any of you are regularly waking up after the sun rises, I'm about to rain on your parade. You are going to have to start waking up earlier. Why? Because the devil and his angels don't sleep in! Don't believe me? Turn on the morning news. While you were getting your beauty rest, the enemy was working overtime. Somebody got shot, someone else was robbed, two people were murdered, there was a car accident with injuries, suicides, drugs, gangs, weapons in schools, homosexuality, rapes, child molestations, teen pregnancies, AIDS, and adultery; do I have to go on? Your family has to go out into a world filled with a myriad of evils, and you are letting them go unprotected because you are in the bed asleep.

"The virtuous wife gets up while it is still dark and prays for her family. She understands that the only way they are going to survive in such a chaotic world is with God on their side, keeping them throughout their daily, individual tasks. Moreover, after she prays for them, she sets the tone for the house. She prepares her family for their day. She gets the house ready for what needs to happen so that they can have a productive day. She takes the meat out the freezer for dinner, she makes the kids lunches, she cooks up a filling breakfast, she decides what chores need to be completed, what bills need to be paid, what activities have to occur that day. By the time the rest of the folks in the house wakes up, their day is already setup for them. No one can complain that they didn't eat breakfast or didn't have clean clothes to wear or that the electricity is off because they forgot to pay the bill. Momma has taken care of everything by getting up early and preparing the way."

Lydia closed her bible and placed it down on the table near her. "A virtuous woman is a preparer. We will talk more about the preparation role of the woman in a future class, but be aware that the man may provide, but it is a woman that prepares. Our man will be in a better position to provide if he is well prepared. If your man is not providing adequately, evaluate whether or not he is best prepared to provide. If he is not adequately prepared, ask yourself is this something you can do to help him become better prepared. It might be praying for him, encouraging him, holding his hand through a difficult process, or maybe just listening to him. Preparation is your role."

After class I walked towards my car in deep thought, barely paying attention to where I was going. I had to admit that I was really starting to feel overwhelmed by this virtuous woman. Getting up at nighttime to pray for her family? Preparing for the day while everyone else enjoyed the comfort of their beds? How was I supposed to do all of that and still have enough energy to run three businesses? I admired her dedication to her family, but did it mean having to give up everything else that mattered to her? I sighed heavily at the thought. Maybe marriage and family just wasn't meant for me.

As I neared my truck and hit the remote to unlock it, I finally dismissed my thoughts and looked up. "What in the world are you doing here?" The words escaped my lips before I could censor them or the tone I spoke them in.

Leaning against my truck as if he owned it and smiling smugly, was the last person I expected to see.

Jonathan Gold.

Lesson 11: Stand For Something or Fall For Anything

The foolish woman is noisy; she is simple and open to all forms of evil, she [willfully and recklessly] knows nothing whatever [of eternal value]. (Proverbs 9:13)

Gold lifted his body up from my vehicle and walked toward me like a man on a mission. "Amber. I thought you'd never come out of that building."

I froze, unable to move anything but my mouth. "What? Wait. Why are you here? What's going on? How did you even know I was here?" The questions poured out of me like pancake batter onto a hot skillet.

"Your business partner slash man, Eric, told me where you were. Or is he your assistant? He answers the phone as if he works for you and not with you. Are you fraternizing, Miss Ross?"

"What Eric and I do is none of your business. What do you want?" In my mind, I saw myself letting Eric have it for telling Gold where I was, but my frustration with him would have to wait until tomorrow and definitely until I figured out why Gold was stalking me at church.

Gold flashed a conceited smile, revealing his pearly-whites. "I want you."

I thought I was losing it. Was Gold flirting with me? It couldn't be. "Excuse me?"

"I said I want you. Yeah, you get under my skin and on my nerves every time I'm around you, but I think that's what turns me on. I figured you out, Ross. You're like the female version of me."

I burst out in laughter. I had to be getting Punk'd. "Is this a joke? Okay, where is the camera? I'm not falling for this so stop playing with me."

Gold ceased smiling and looked at me as if I was the crazy one. That was when I realized that he was serious. This wasn't a game. He really was trying to hit on me.

"You're serious?" I asked in amazement. Talk about a switch-a-roo!

Taking another step closer to me, he reduced the distance between us. "One thing you should already know about me, Ross, is that I don't play games."

I took a step backwards, increasing the space between us once again. "Okay, let me get this straight. You called my office and found out where to find me so that you could tell me that you want to be with me? Like romantically?"

"Basically." He stepped forward again. "You know, you are really a beautiful woman."

This guy was amazing! He really thought he was Rico Suave or better yet, Denzel or Billy Dee! "When did you decide all of this? I thought you hated me. What about the jokes about me not having a man or owning a dress, and blah, blah, blah?"

He took another step closer to me. "Like you, I was trying to deny my feelings for you, but when I saw you on the boat, in that dress, with your 'man-boy' assistant, I knew we were meant to be."

I rested my right hand on my hip and rolled my neck. "Okay, first of all, his name is Eric, and he is not my assistant. Secondly, whoa! We were meant to be? I can't believe this is happening!" I threw both my hands up in distress.

"Believe it. Come on, Amber. You and I make sense. We are both influential people in the business world, we both have money and good looks; we're the perfect couple. We're a power couple like Barack and Michelle."

"Did you really just compare me and you to Barack and Michelle Obama? This is so crazy! You are so crazy! Are you on medication or something? Do you have a mental illness I don't know about with the exception of Narcissistic Personality Disorder? Maybe a little Bipolar or Dissociative Identity going on? You are really freaking me out."

He reached out and grabbed my left hand. "Baby, stop fighting it."

I looked suspiciously into his eyes. "Baby?"

He licked his lips seductively. "Amber. Sweetheart. It's like this. I know I am the best thing that's ever going to happen to you. I mean, seriously, what man do you know that can compliment you like I can? Eric? I doubt that. Be honest. Are you guys really together? Is it really that serious?"

I quickly broke eye contact, forcing myself to gaze out into the distance. In my mind he was a pompous, arrogant, sexist idiot, but he was also right. He was a male version of me. He was just as ambitious and aggressive as I was. We hated each other because we were mirrors of each other. The realization of our similarities made me feel nauseous. "I...I don't want to talk about Eric. Listen, I really am surprised by your confession. I totally need to go home and get some sleep because I can't think straight right now."

He kissed my hand lightly. "Okay, I can respect that. But at least let me take you out on a date."

A date with Gold? When pigs fly! "Absolutely not! Gold, I–"

"You can't make the right decision if you haven't even given me a fair chance. Am I right?" He rubbed my hand gently before letting it go.

I wanted to continue being cold towards him and tell him to go jump off a bridge, kick rocks, or something dreadful, but to my dismay, I felt myself caving in. Was this another time when I needed to let men be men? I couldn't stand Gold, but I also couldn't help being flattered by his pursuit. "I...I guess. Okay. *One date.* That's it!" I couldn't believe I was agreeing to a date with my archenemy. I must have been losing my edge...and my mind.

"Great. I'll pick you up from your office tomorrow at 5 o'clock," he said as he turned and walked away.

His words played slowly through my mind. Five o'clock. Tomorrow. Pick me up at my office. My heart skipped a beat. Oh no, Eric. "No, no, no! You can't–," I started to yell out to him, but he had already jumped in his Hummer and was pulling off.

"Great! Just great!" I mumbled aloud. I started to mock him, "Amber I want you, you're a beautiful woman," but I realized I was still standing outside in the parking lot and probably looked cuckoo. At least my behavior was mimicking my feelings. Argh!

The next day I planned to sit down and talk with Eric before Gold showed up for our date. I didn't want Eric to be offended, but somehow the day got away from me and before I knew it, five o'clock had arrived, Gold was sitting in the lobby, and Eric was looking bewildered.

"You have a visitor, Boss. That guy Mr. Gold. He also called here last night looking for you. Said it was important," Eric stated as he stood at the entrance to my office and poked his head inside.

"Yes, and thanks to you, Eric, he showed up at my church." I didn't mean to come off as hostile, but I was still a little salty about the whole situation.

Eric lowered his eyes apologetically. "Sorry. I thought it might be something critical related to the Green Global venture. So what's he doing here now?"

How could I tell Eric I was going out on a date with Gold? Eric was the one who saved me from total humiliation in Savannah, so hobnobbing with the enemy did not look good on my part. Not at all; however, I also didn't want to lie to him. Eric was a good guy. He deserved my honesty, for he sincerely liked me. I still hadn't decided whether or not I wanted to date him. The truth was I didn't trust myself around him. At least Gold annoyed me so I wasn't worried about falling in love or getting hurt by him. But Eric...Eric was a heartbreak waiting to happen. I could feel it. I really needed to be honest with him.

"Uh...Gold and I are...going out to dinner," I said weakly.

"Dinner? As in a date?" Eric glared at me as if I had just told him he was being fired for insubordination. I was hurting him, which was the last thing I wanted to do.

"Dinner as in a business dinner," I lied without thinking.

His facial expression turned into relief. "Oh. Yeah, that makes sense. That's what I…Well, I don't want to make you late for your meeting." He smiled at me and walked back up towards the lobby, more than likely delivering a message to Gold that I was on my way.

I sighed, feeling extremely guilty about lying to Eric. I would have to make it up to him somehow.

On my way toward the lobby, I stuck my head into Eric's office. He still looked a little frazzled, which made me feel even more ashamed.

"Hey," I said, feigning a cheerful spirit. "I haven't forgotten about what you said to me. I'm still mulling it over. Why don't we hang out this weekend, you know, get to know each other better? Maybe a movie or something?"

His eyes lit up. "Yeah, that sounds nice. There's actually a Reggae concert on Friday night that my fraternity is hosting. Maybe you'd like to go with me."

"I didn't know you were in a fraternity."

He smiled, proudly. "Yeah. Phi Beta Sigma. I pledged my sophomore year in college. I dropped out of school during my junior year, but I still remained active with my frat. I just don't wear a bunch of paraphernalia like other people do."

"I see. Well, Friday it is then. I'd better get going." I waved bye and quickly made my way to the lobby where Gold was impatiently walking back and forth. When he looked up and saw me coming in his direction, a confident grin overtook his face, replacing the irritated scowl.

"Ready?" I asked, wanting to get out of there before Eric saw or heard too much. I had somehow managed to set up two dates in the same week with two different guys, and at that moment, they were both in the same building!

Gold allowed his eyes to roam my body and then ran his hand down the back of his neck. I could only imagine the sinful thoughts he was having at my expense. "The question is are you ready?" he asked.

I refused to respond to him. Instead, I bit my lip and walked out of the front door, gesturing for him to follow. This was going to be a long night.

Surprisingly, dinner with Gold turned out better than I had imagined. He took me to a ritzy Tapas restaurant in Buckhead that seemed to promote small portions and exorbitant prices. I was glad that he was picking up the tab because, although I wasn't cheap, I also didn't believe in being flashy. Gold, on the other hand, was doing the whole wine-and-dine thing, trying to win me over with charisma and the good old "money is no object" line.

I had to confess, it was nice to go out with a man who could afford me. Chris had a pretty decent job; he worked for the federal government's department of revenue, but his $70K job was less than a third of my annual income. In addition, Chris had too many bills. He was living beyond his means, and after he paid his mortgage, car note, and whatnot, he could barely afford to buy me a new Coach bag. And Eric. Eric made less than Chris, a lot less. I didn't know what he was doing with his money, but with a child to care for, I was sure that his funds were tight. Gold, however, could buy me a diamond engagement ring at that very moment and not blink. Wasn't that the type of man I needed?

As we ate and enjoyed the dimly lit restaurant, various associates of Gold's came to our table to wish us well. Gold, proud to have me on his arm, boastfully introduced me as one of the most successful women in Atlanta and his future wife.

Gold and I married? This was just the first date. How did I go from "You probably don't have a man" to "The next Mrs. Gold"? What in tarnation was going on?

"Wow! You must really be an amazing woman to have Jonathan Gold talking about marriage," one of his friends responded as he cased me with his eyes.

"Well, marriage is a bit premature to discuss, but yes, I would say I am an amazing woman," I shamelessly replied.

The guy looked at me, then back at Gold, and let out a loud chuckle. "Yeah, she's the one, Jon! Don't let her slip away! She's definitely the female version of you."

Okay, now I was offended. When Gold said that I was the female version of him, I thought the statement had some level of validity. Now, the comment coming from someone who didn't know me from a can of paint, I couldn't help but feel like someone had called me the equivalent of the "B" word. Gold's social skills were like drinking lemonade without sugar, awful and bitter, so if I was Gold in a pair of heels and a skirt, I must be pretty bad.

I wanted to be depressed, but it was hard with Gold whispering sweet nothings in my ear. After the self-esteem blow of basically being called a self-absorbed jerk by Gold's friend, I really needed an ego boost, and Gold was saying all of the right things. By the end of the night, I still didn't trust him, but I respected him enough to agree to a second date on Saturday. Was I a glutton for pain or what?

Friday came before I could get my head wrapped around this thing about dating Gold and Eric simultaneously. Gold was sending me flowers to the office and calling daily like he had already proposed and the wedding date had been set. Eric was heated by the notion that Gold might be his competition, but I assured him that Gold was just trying to make-up for being such a prick to me during our business dealings. Another lie. I would have to do a whole lot of praying and asking God for forgiveness.

As much as I wasn't the kind of girl to play around with men, I inwardly loved all of the attention. I hadn't gotten this much action since college. The idea of two handsome brothas scrapping over me made me a little giddy. Maybe this Wife 101 class was really working…Well, I'm sure that God wasn't too happy about me playing the field, but how would I know which one was best for me if I didn't test drive both of them first?

Eric had come to work in his usual business casual attire, but by the end of the day had changed into a blue and white collegiate sweater with Phi Beta Sigma's Greek letters sprawled down the front, right side of it and a pair of blue jeans. Catching the hint, I also changed out of my black suit into a grey sweater and a matching pair of leggings. We left from the office together and rode in his Impala to the event.

The concert was being held at a community center in downtown Decatur. By the time we got there, the place was packed, but Eric had asked a few of his frat brothers saved us seats in the front row so we weren't worried about the crowd. The auditorium was nicely decorated with blue and white balloons, candles, and streamers, giving the normally indifferent location a festive feel.

Three reggae acts performed during the course of the night, bringing the crowd to its knees in overwhelming approval. Hanging with Eric was so enjoyable, just like my experience with him in Savannah. I felt comfortable with him as if I had known him my whole life. I loved how much I could be myself with him, but that was also the part that bothered me about him. I was so relaxed with him that the fireworks seemed to be missing. I didn't get that spark, those butterflies in my stomach when I was around him. I wasn't nervous or anxious, I just felt at ease. Was that normal? Should I feel more?

I was pondering the absence of butterflies at the end of the concert when to my disbelief, I felt the spark I'd been waiting to feel, but Eric was not the source.

Walking toward me in all of his grandeur was none other than Chris. He looked good, really good. His eyes seemed to twinkle in anticipation. I could smell his Polo cologne even from a distance. All of the emotions for him that I had been repressing were bubbling in my chest, threatening to resurface. I'll say it again: what in tarnation was going on?

Thankfully, Eric was conversing with a few of his frat brothers when Chris approached me, or else he would have really hit the roof.

"Hey you," Chris said flirtatiously.

I looked around myself to make sure he wasn't speaking to someone else. "You talking to me?" I asked quizzically.

He laughed. I'm glad someone was amused because I wasn't. "Of course," he said. "Who else would I be talking to?"

I sucked my teeth. "Your wife, Seasons' Greetings, Merry Christmas, or whatever her name is."

"I see you still got jokes. Noel, it's Noel, and we're not married."

"Why not? I thought you all were *in love*." My sarcastic attitude wasn't going unnoticed.

He nodded his head as if to say he deserved my iciness. "Things haven't been working out the way we expected. We're kind of taking some time to think the relationship over."

I knew his break-up with Noel shouldn't have mattered, but hearing about it made me feel a lot better. "I see, so what are you doing here?"

"My boy told me about this thing. What about you? Are you on a date?"

It was my chance to sucker punch him, and I intended to hit him hard. "Actually I am on a date with a wonderful man."

He shifted his weight from one foot to the other. "Is it serious, I mean, with this dude?"

I smiled at his insecurity. "Maybe. We're considering our options."

He stared at me for a moment before asking, "Can I call you?"

I almost choked on my own saliva. "What? No!"

He sweetly brushed my hair away from my eyes with his hand. "Do you still love me?"

"You must have bumped your head."

"I think you do." He moved a step closer to me and whispered in my ear, "I miss you."

My heart was beating a million times a minute. My esophagus felt like it was closing up, and I was sure that if I didn't walk away soon, I was going to straight pass out or have a panic attack. "Okay...I'm going to go because, yeah, I think my date is...you're trippin'."

"I'm gonna call you."

"Please don't."

"I'll talk to you soon. Probably tonight."

I threw him a nasty look and rushed away to find Eric. An hour later, I was changing into my pajamas when my cell phone rang. I looked at the screen in fear.

It was Chris. I sent it to voicemail. He left a message.

Hi Amber, it's Chris. I told you I would call. I meant what I said today. I really miss you. You looked so stunning tonight. Whatever you're doing, keep it up. Anyway, call me as soon as you can.

I thought I was over Chris, well, mostly over him. Now the wacky emotions I was experiencing told me loud and clear that Chris was definitely still in my system. With everything else going on, I did not even want to think about adding Chris to the equation. *God, I really, really, really, don't understand!*

Three guys in one week. I was convinced that the Wife 101 class was dangerous.

Lesson 12: Know When to Say No

She considers a [new] field before she buys or accepts it [expanding prudently and not courting neglect of her present duties by assuming other duties]; with her savings [of time and strength] she plants fruitful vines in her vineyard. She girds herself with strength [spiritual, mental, and physical fitness for her God-given task] and makes her arms strong and firm. (Proverbs 31:16-17)

Saturday's date with Gold was another charming experience. He took me to an Off-Broadway performance of *Les Misérables*. Although he was still the arrogant, chauvinist that annoyed me, I was starting to appreciate letting a man do all of the hard work. It felt good to be pampered. It was a relief to go somewhere fancy and not worry about who was going to pay, or how I was going to adjust my budget to cover an indulgence. Yes, I had a nice financial cushion, but one of the reasons I had the dough was because I knew how to bargain and save. Gold seemed to get a kick out of spending excessively; who was I to stop him?

As I sat in my next Wife 101 class, I tried hard to focus on Lydia's wisdom and not my own personal drama. I had been praying a lot for guidance, hoping God's will for me would become obvious, but the more time went by, the more confused I felt. Chris had called me several times, and although I had yet to answer his calls, I knew I would have to face him eventually. Eric had also been calling periodically to check up on me. Unlike Chris and Gold, Eric wasn't as aggressive. He showed his interest, but then backed up and gave me space to breathe and think. At this point, I wasn't sure if his relaxed approach was a turn on or a turn off. Like most women, I wanted attention and to feel loved, even if I said otherwise.

"One of the most common flaws a giving woman has is the inability to say no," Lydia stated, earning my complete attention. "Giving people tend to be people pleasers. We feel obligated to help others and feel bad when or if we have to turn them down. Because of this, many women are overextended. We may have a fulltime job along with our wife and parenting roles, but on top of that, we have committed ourselves to a bunch of other activities and roles both inside and outside of the church. We may be on the usher board, in the choir, helping with the youth ministry or a bake sale; we may be a community leader, on the PTA, Girl Scout troop leader, a soccer mom, book club president, on the neighborhood watch, or a bunch of other roles. I am sure you can add your activities to the list. The point is that we get to a place where we are so stretched that it is impossible to do everything, and in the process, we begin to neglect our most important roles."

A few women in the class nodded, and two or three yelled out, "Amen."

Lydia continued, "I call this the Superwoman Syndrome. So many of us are walking around here with the letter S on our chests. Although you think you can do everything, the enemy is wreaking havoc around you because you've left holes. Your family is neglected, your friends are neglected, you are neglected, your husband is neglected, and most importantly, your God is neglected. You are so busy trying to impress this and that committee or group, who in the scope of things are unimportant, that the ones who really matter don't have access to you. Then you find yourself perplexed when your husband leaves you for another woman, your kids end up hanging with the wrong crowd, your friends don't answer your calls anymore, and your own health is deteriorating.

"Proverbs 31:16 says, 'She considers a new field before she buys or accepts it, expanding prudently and not courting neglect of her present duties by assuming other duties; with her savings of time and strength she plants fruitful vines in her vineyard.' This statement goes back to our conversation about time and how much of it you do or don't have. For this reason, it is important to review your list of hours and how you spend your day. Pull out your list of activities and hours and let's look at them."

We all followed her instructions and took out our activities lists.

"If you are already overspent on hours, ask yourself why. Is it because you said yes to some things you should have said no to? And if you are overspent, what or who is being neglected?"

Every woman in the class wore an expression of guilt. Even I, with no children or husband, knew the finger of error was pointed at me. I always overcommitted myself and then became frustrated when I was worn out and exhausted. Truthfully, I was probably over committing myself at the moment by dating two men at the same time, but I wasn't sure how to cut either of them off without missing out on a potential love connection.

Lydia gathered her well used bible into her arms. "Verse sixteen tells us that we should be careful when it comes to accepting or taking on new things. We first have to make sure we have room in our lives for these new things. If we don't, we must say no until we have adjusted ourselves and can take on something else without it causing us to neglect what is already in our lives.

"The verse then goes on to say that because she is not overspent on time and energy, she can take the additional time and energy she has and make the most out of what she is doing. She is not just throwing dinner together; she is making hearty meals. She is not giving God a two minute prayer' she is taking sufficient time to talk with Him and letting Him lead her. She is not too busy to help her kids with their homework, go to the parent-teacher conference, or attend their sports game. She is not too busy to pull her hair together, make sure her clothes are ironed, or put some lotion on her feet. She rarely tells her husband that she can't attend his office party with him or cuddle up with him at night. She has the time and energy to do what she does well. How many of us can say the same?"

I smiled to myself. If I were married, the former would describe me all of the way! I could see it now, me telling my husband I can't do something with him because I'm working. She definitely had my number! I would most certainly have to work on better management of my schedule before I married.

"Ladies, ever since I learned the significance of verse sixteen, it continues to replay itself in my ear over and over again," Lydia said, shaking her head in the process. "Some of us have purchased way too many fields without considering the ones we already have. 'Sure, I'll join this committee!' or 'Yes, I'll do this for a friend!' or 'No problem, I can handle that too!' That is what we sound like as we buy fields. The problem is that we already have way too much going on. Do you realize how much time it takes alone to keep your house cleaned and to cook a hot meal a few times a week? How can you effectively take care of home if you are always obligating yourself to other people and things? What is worse is that the first thing that usually suffers is your relationship with God. It is so hard to hear from God when you are overwhelmed.

"We have to learn to stop, think, pray on these things, and often say no. And not feel bad. Why should we feel bad when we are being honest with ourselves and others about what we can realistically handle? We would rather kill ourselves and neglect the most important people and things in our lives than turn someone or something down. Why? Because we are trying to please people rather than please God."

I was so guilty of taking on too much at times in efforts to please others. I guess I just wanted to come across as dependable, professional, and capable. I wanted others to see me in a positive light, to regard me highly, but like Lydia was saying, in the process, I was overwhelming myself and neglecting other important aspects of my life. I had a housekeeper cleaning my house twice a month because I didn't have the time to do it myself. What woman doesn't clean her own home? Better yet, what man wants a woman who doesn't have the time to clean her own home? Many wives have lost their husbands to housekeepers and nannies!

I didn't have the time or energy to cook so I practically ate out every day. I needed a manicure so badly that I expected any day now for my fingernails to just give up on me and fall off. The only reason my relationship with God was halfway in a good place was because of this class, but before that, my prayer life and one-on-one time was nonexistent. Everyone else's needs around me were being taken care of because I was so focused on pleasing people. I would have to make some changes, start taking out some time for myself, and stop over obligating myself.

Lydia placed her free hand on her hip. "Now before I continue on, I know some of you may be thinking, if a woman is doing all of this, what is her man doing? That is one of our downfalls, ladies. We are always worried about what someone else is doing in comparison to us. Don't worry about what he is or isn't doing. Your job is to do what you are supposed to do. If you were at work, would you stop doing your job because a coworker wasn't doing theirs? If so, both of you are going to end up jobless! Do your part. Most times when you do your part, you inspire others to do theirs. When I was in college, I noticed that when my friends studied, I was motivated to study, too. If you do your part as a wife, your husband may be motivated to do his. If he isn't inspired by you, pray for him and let God work out the details."

Lydia glanced down at her open notebook which was lying on a table in the front of the classroom. "Looking at the verse from the literal perspective, we can also dissect that this woman is not a spendthrift. I may step on a few toes with this one, but that's alright; I do step on them in love. The fact that she considers what she is purchasing before she buys suggests that she makes careful and cautious money decisions. She can be trusted with the family's money because she is not going to waste it overspending or buying unnecessary things. Many of us can take a lesson from this woman when it comes to our spending habits. If you are in debt because you're living beyond your means, this verse is for you. Why go out and get a new car loan when you have a perfectly good old car that is paid off sitting in your driveway? Why talk your husband into buying an expensive new house if you all have to work two or three jobs just to pay the monthly mortgage? The virtuous woman is not trying to keep up with the Joneses or impress other folks. She is wise in her spending and because she is, she has extra leftover to make what she has the very best it can be."

Amen to that sister, I thought. *Finally, something I am already doing right.* I believed in the old saying, "Money saved is money earned" and I loved to earn money!

"Moving on to verse seventeen: 'She girds herself with strength, spiritual, mental, and physical fitness for her God-given task, and makes her arms strong and firm.' This is not a weak woman. She is physically, mentally, and spiritually strong, understanding that she will need vigor in all three areas to fulfill her tasks. You need more than just physical energy to raise children; you need mental and spiritual power as well. To be successful in marriage, you can't just be spiritually strong; you need mental and physical strength also. To handle your work day, you require more than just mental sharpness; you need spiritual and physical acuity, too.

"If you are someone who goes to the gym regularly, make sure you don't forget to train your mind and your spirit as well. If you are someone always in church or always reading the Word, make sure to empower yourself mentally and physically, too. If you are highly educated and love to learn, don't overlook your spirit or your body. It takes wholeness of self to be the fruitful woman God is calling you to be."

I left class feeling invigorated. Yeah, I still wasn't sure what I would do about Eric and Gold, but I knew I needed to make a wise choice and to make it soon. I thought about taking a day or two off and doing something to clear my head. After mulling over needing a break for a few minutes, I decided taking some time off was a great idea, and even better, I knew exactly what I could do. I hadn't been to the spa in forever, and lately, I hadn't spent much time with Tisha either. The spa and spending time with Tisha would be the perfect way to follow through on my new pledge to take better care of myself. Thankfully, it was February recess for schools, and Tisha was off for the week. Riding down I-20, I dialed her number and waited for her to pick up.

"Hello Stranger," she answered sarcastically.

"I know. I'm sorry, but I have the perfect way to make it up to you!"

"I'm listening."

"How about you and me do a spa day tomorrow, my treat?"

"How about…yes!" she screamed.

I laughed. "Cool. I'll go make the appointment online tonight and call you back to tell you what time to be ready. Hot stone or deep tissue?"

"You know I want the hot stone massage. And see if we can get pedicures. My toes are looking real crusty."

"Too much information!" I laughed again. "Don't tell anybody, but mine are too! Wait. Since we are spending *my* money, I'll get one of those day packages where you get like the massage, facial, pedicure, manicure, and lunch for one price. Girl, I've got tons to tell you."

"Ooh! Sounds juicy! Is it related to the opposite sex?" Tisha was always one for good gossip.

"Yes. You will never believe the past few weeks I've had. And guess who's stalking me now."

"Who?"

"Your boy Chris!"

"Shut up!"

"No joke. I'll tell you about it all tomorrow when I can tell you the whole story in detail. I'll text you the spa info tonight when I get home."

Lesson 13: Make a Bed You Are Willing to Lie In

Every wise woman builds her house, but the foolish one tears it down with her own hands. (Proverbs 14:1)

It was 1:30 p.m. on Tuesday, and Tisha and I were lounging by an indoor pool, eating tuna sandwiches and fruit salad at Pecan Creek Day Spa. We had already received our seaweed body wraps and hot stone therapy massages and were now having a light lunch before getting manis and pedis at 2 o'clock. Our final services for the day were peppermint and citrus facials at 3 p.m.

I was already grateful that I had decided to play hooky from work and do a day at the spa. My entire body felt relaxed. My masseuse Loni had expertly worked out every kink and knot in my shoulders and back. Tisha was equally appreciative, expressing her bliss as she spooned a pineapple chunk into her mouth. "Girl! This is what I am talking about! I'm so glad you set this up. I didn't realize how much I needed a little R&R."

I wiped my mouth with a thick, cloth napkin. "Ditto. I'm almost tempted to make another appointment for tomorrow. Lord knows how much my spine needs some love."

"Right. We have to promise to do this at least once a month. We work hard. We deserve a little pampering."

"That's for sure. The way I'm feeling right now, I'm ready to kidnap Loni, gag her, throw her into the trunk, and take her home with me. I desperately need a live in masseuse. Do you think they would notice that she was missing?"

Tisha giggled. "Yes, but don't tell me your plan because then it makes me an accomplice...You're crazy! So you know I'm on pins and needles waiting to hear about Chris and whatever drama you've got going on. I've been patient, but I can't wait any longer. Spill it."

I took a swig of the unsweetened iced tea we'd been given with our lunch. I had tried to doctor it up with a zillion sugar packets, but it still tasted bland. "Well, it's kind of complex. Basically, I'm sort of dating two guys right now."

Tisha shrieked. "You're dating Chris again?"

"No! Not him. However, I was on a date with one of the guys last week, and I ran into Chris. He was looking sooo good! It was so hard to play unaffected, but I think I handled myself well. He was like asking me if I was on a date and telling me that him and that chick aren't getting married anymore."

"For real?"

"Yes. Then he asks me if I still love him, and you know I was trying not to go there with him!"

"I know that's right!" We gave each other a high five and laughed.

"Then he was telling me that he misses me and says he is going to call me. He did call that night, but I didn't answer. Sent it straight to voicemail!"

"You can leave a message after the beep." Tisha impersonated the robotic voice that came standard on most voicemails.

"Beep!" I chimed before we fell out laughing. I was laughing so hard, my eyes began to water. Wiping away the moisture from my eyes, I continued, "He's been calling ever since. I still haven't returned his calls yet."

Tisha leaned back in the padded wicker chair. "Why not?"

I sipped on my ice tea again, considering my thoughts before replying. "Because I think I still have feelings for him, and I don't want to go back to being played again."

"But what if he's sincere? What if being with this other woman has made him realize how much he messed up with you?"

"I've thought about that, but I don't know. And then there's Gold and Eric to think about."

Tisha sat up straight. "Gold and Eric? You mean Eric, your employee Eric from Valentine's Day? And Gold as in the business-partner-from-hell Gold?"

"Yes and yes," I responded in an innocent childlike voice.

Her eyes narrowed as if I had deceived her. "I knew something was going on between you and Eric. I saw it in his eyes that night. You all over there trying to act all brand new. Don't sleep on your girl! I should have been a private detective. My name would have been P.I.T. short for Private Investigator Tisha, or short for Pit Bull, or even Pretty Intelligent Thing like Michael Jackson's PYT."

I looked at her like she was nutting up. Tisha was a known scatterbrain.

She refocused. "So this thing with Gold? When did that happen?"

I placed the empty glass down on the glass, bistro style table. "Actually when you ask me about Eric, there really was nothing. It wasn't until he dropped me off that night that he told me how he felt. As for Gold, he just showed up to my church like a week ago claiming he wants to be with me. I really thought it was a joke, but we've been out a couple times, and this guy is serious."

"Amber the player! What? Hell must have frozen over," Tisha taunted.

"I know! You know me. This is not my style. I feel sort of bad. I wasn't trying to play the field, but they all came at me at once. I think it's this class I'm taking..." I hadn't meant to let the cat out the bag yet. Not that the class was a big secret, but I wanted to see it through first before letting Tisha in on it.

"What class?"

It was time to come clean. I bit my lip. "There's a class at my church called Wife 101 that I've been taking since the whole engagement party thing. We're studying Proverbs 31, you know, the whole virtuous woman chapter. It's really interesting, and I have to say I've learned a lot."

"Like what?" Tisha was morphing into her interrogation mode which was never a good sign.

"Like if I want to be married, I'm going to have to make a lot of changes. I'm starting to understand why men never saw me as wife material. I've been living the life of a man rather than a woman. I mean, I love what I've accomplished, but what man wants a woman who he always has to compete with?"

"Obviously three: Chris, Eric, and Gold," she confidently replied as she counted them out on her fingers.

I sighed. "Maybe, but I think all this attention is coming from the fact that I've been praying and asking God to help make me a better woman."

"Mm. Why didn't you tell me about this class? I would have taken it with you."

"Because I know you. You would have been like, 'I don't need no class to tell me how to get a man!' I figured that if I tried it and liked it I could tell you about it later."

She peered at me suspiciously and then waved me off. "Yeah, you know me. I would have probably said something smart. So what are you thinking about these men in your life. Do you think one of these dudes is *the one*?"

I smiled; glad Tisha had taken the news well. She was known for making a mountain out of a molehill. "Girl, your guess is better than mine. Eric is really sweet, but I don't feel the fireworks with him. I think he's really cute and very respectful, but it's like were best friends rather than a couple. You know what I mean?"

Tisha rolled her eyes, obviously not feeling the idea of me and Eric. "Mm Hmm. Well, you can't force it if it's not there. Anyway, can you honestly be with someone who works for you? How much money does he make? $30K? He's an office manager. Sweet or not, you could do so much better. And doesn't he have a kid. Three words: baby momma drama!"

I snickered. "Quite possibly. You might be right, and you know I ain't trying to have to knock a chick out for running up on me over the father of her child."

"Exactly! That's why I have a strict no children rule. I don't do guys with kids unless A, his kids are grown or B, his baby momma is married to someone else. Eric should have a big, red X over his name and face."

I shrugged. "Well, Gold is the exact opposite of Eric. He still irritates me with all of his pride and ego, but he spends money on me like it's going out of style. He knows everybody who is somebody, and he tells everyone that I'm his future wife. He says we would be a power couple, that I'm the female version of him; he even compared us to Barack and Michelle Obama. He is so convinced that we're meant to be."

Tisha grinned. "Maybe you are."

"There are definitely benefits to being with him, but I wonder if I could ever really be in love with him. It kind of feels like it would all be superficial. Money, parties, politics, blah, blah, blah. Nothing real. Maybe I'm thinking too deeply about it."

"Mmm. Girl, just enjoy it while it lasts…So what about Chris?"

"What about him?"

"Second chance?"

"Should I?"

She smirked deviously. "You should. At least to see if the feelings are still there. Some people gotta break up to make up, if you get my drift. I say call him; you never know."

After talking with Tisha, I was on the verge of making some decisions. As much as I was fond of Eric, I wasn't sure he was right for me. I didn't want to reject him, but somehow I had to let him know that I just wanted to remain friends. I also was planning on calling Chris. I wasn't sure about allowing him back into my life, but I was at least willing to let him plead his case.

I decided to take Eric out for lunch on Thursday to give him the bad news. I opted for the Japanese Hibachi at *Benihana's*, one of my favorite restaurants. I figured the impromptu entertainment from the chef cooking in front of us would make it easier to dish out the "just friends" speech.

The others at our table and I marveled at our chef for turning a sliced up onion into a smoking volcano, Eric threw me for a loop. He asked about my family.

"I hope I'm not overstepping my boundaries, but I was hoping you would tell me about your family. You've never mentioned your parents or siblings before. Are they here in Atlanta?" he asked as the others around us clapped for the chef.

I blinked twice. "No. They're back in New York, where I'm from."

He raised his eyebrows in shock. "You're from New York? I didn't know that. You don't sound like a Yankee."

"Yeah, born and raised. Long Island. I guess when I went off to college I lost a bit of my accent."

"You ever go back to visit?"

"No, not really. I haven't been home in…like five or six years."

"You don't miss your folks?"

I shifted a bit in my seat. "Honestly, no…I never really knew my real father. He died when I was a baby." I looked away from Eric and watched the chef as I continued to speak, "When I was seven, my mom married this guy named Otis. They've been together ever since. I've got a younger brother named Alex. Otis is his father."

"You say that like you don't care much for your stepfather."

I could feel Eric's eyes on me, but I refused to make eye contact with him. Talking about my family had always been a touchy subject for me. "I don't; that's why I call him Otis and not my stepfather. Otis wasn't abusive or anything, but he wasn't the greatest husband or father. He acted as if his little financial contribution to the household gave him the right to run my mother's life. He had to be in control over everything, all the time. I never understood why my mother thought she needed him."

"What's your mom's name?"

I glanced at Eric and smiled. "Anita. I really love my mom, but she frustrates me so much…She reminds me of the kind of woman I don't want to be."

"And what's that?"

"Co-dependent…Thinking about it, I guess that's why I work so hard to have my own. I don't want to feel like I need to be with someone to survive."

"That helps me understand you so much better. Just so you know, you're not co-dependent. Actually you may be the most non-co-dependent woman I know," Eric chuckled.

"Hush!" I pushed his arm, playfully. "Sorry if this conversation is ruining your mood."

He patted my leg. "No, I asked, and I appreciate you opening up to me. You probably don't share that with most people, so I feel special."

I looked away again, watching the chef scoop large portions of fried rice onto our plates. "You're right; I don't tell people about my family, but not because it's a secret. Really, most people don't ask. I guess they don't care."

"I care. How can I know you if I don't know your past? Our families may not be perfect, but they're a part of us, of who we become."

I nodded. That was what I liked about Eric; I could talk to him about anything. He made me feel comfortable and accepted. As much as the fireworks were still missing, I wasn't ready just yet to put him into the "friends only" category. "So, what about you? Where are your people?" I asked before attempting to eat fried rice using chopsticks.

"We're all here in Atlanta. I've got two sisters and a brother; I'm the youngest. My parents live out in Conyers. Maybe I'll take you out there to meet them one day, if you act right."

"Act right?"

He laughed. "Yeah! I can't bring you around my momma if you don't have home training. My mother does not play that!"

"Whatever!" I jokingly shoved his arm again. I looked into his genuine eyes and knew I couldn't tell him that I didn't want to date him. Something within me, a small inner voice, begged me not to cut him off. Not so fast.

That night, following Tisha's advice, I finally decided to answer Chris' call.

"H-H-Hello, Amber?" he stammered, obviously surprised that I actually picked up the phone after a week of sending his calls to my voicemail.

"Yeah. What's up Chris?" I asked dryly, still unsure of how I felt about reconnecting with him. During the year that we'd dated, I had grown to have strong feelings for him, possibly love him. I had told him that I loved him a thousand times, but now in hindsight I wondered if it was real love or some form of deep infatuation. I really thought we had a chance of making it, of turning our budding romance into marriage. I should have read the signs when he was resistant to discussing anything related to weddings or long-term commitment. He claimed that he was still trying to find himself, still trying to get himself together, whatever that meant. When he disappeared without a "Dear John" letter or anything, I was completely floored. I knew he was a little unstable, but how does someone make you care about them then just vanish into thin air? I had never been the type of woman to fall apart over a man, but I did have a few depressed days over Chris. Well, more than a few, more like several...okay, a month. So, when he showed up out of nowhere talking about marrying someone else, I was hurt more than I let on. It was like getting stabbed in the back. Then just when I was trying to move forward with my life, here he was again! So yes, I was very apprehensive about answering his calls.

"I-I can't believe you actually picked up. I thought I was going to have to come by your office just to get you to talk to me."

Although he couldn't see me, I rolled my eyes. "Please don't come to my business. You know how I am about bringing personal drama to the workplace."

He sighed heavily. "So that's how you see me now? As drama?"

"Yes, drama is the perfect word to describe you."

"Okay, I guess I deserve that one. So...how have you been?"

Aggravated, I sucked my teeth. "I'm blessed as always. Look, let's not beat around the bush. You evidently want something based on the fact that you've called me 2-3 times a day for the past week. So say what you need to say because I have things to do."

"I guess I deserve that one, too…Amber, let me start by saying that I'm sorry. I know I've hurt you, and I truly apologize for anything that I've done to cause you pain. I'm not calling to cause you any problems. I just really miss you, and I was hoping that we could sort of start over, you know, hang out again."

"Start over?"

"Yeah. We had something good. I think we could get it back to the way it used to be."

"The way it used to be?"

He let out a nervous snicker. "Yes, the way it used to be. Why do you keep repeating everything I say?"

He had some nerve! I couldn't believe he was coming at me as if everything was peaches and roses between us. Did he think I was a fool? I was beyond offended. "Because, Chris, you can't just call a woman after breaking her heart and say let's start over. I have feelings, Chris. You can't just play with them whenever it's convenient for you. You are so selfish."

"So you don't miss us? Tell me you don't and I'll leave you alone."

I laughed, but not because anything was funny. He was ridiculous. This conversation was ridiculous! Why did I ever listen to Tisha? Exasperated, I said, "I don't!"

"See, Amber, I know that's not true. I could see it in your eyes when I saw you last week. Come on; be honest with me, baby. Be honest with yourself."

By this point I was so mad, I was seething. He wasn't listening to me. Ugh! "No, why don't you be honest, Chris. What's the real reason why you're back in my face? What really happened with you and Noel?"

He snickered again. "I think that's the first time you got her name right."

"I know her name, Chris. That's beside the point. Why aren't you two getting married? Keep it real."

"I am keeping it real. I told you, we were moving too fast. We really didn't know each other as well as we thought. We talked about it and decided to back up from each other for a while."

"And so now that your perfect woman doesn't want you, you're settling for the next best thing with me? I don't think so."

"That's not what it is, Amber."

"That's sure what it looks like." He really didn't seem to get it. It wasn't that I didn't care about him, but I couldn't keep playing myself! "How do I know that she won't call you a week or month from now, and you won't leave me high and dry again?"

"That's not going to happen."

"How do I know?"

"Because I told you it won't."

"That's not enough! You told me that you cared about me and that you were there for me, but you still left me. I don't trust you, Chris, and it's all your fault."

He got quiet for a second which gave me a moment to recollect myself. I was about to hang up on him when he exhaled loudly and said, "You're right. I messed up, but I'm willing to do what it takes to make things between us good again. Give me a chance. Everyone deserves another chance. Come on; you're a Christian. Isn't that what Jesus is all about, forgiveness and giving us another chance? Don't be like everybody else, don't be a hypocrite; say one thing and do another. So many church folks want God to forgive them, but then won't forgive anyone else. I know you're not like that, Amber. You've got a big heart and a lot of love. I really need a little piece of that love right now. Just a chance, that's all I'm asking for. Just a little forgiveness."

I was tired, but I couldn't argue with him. Most women would have never answered the phone, but I did because inside, I truly wanted to forgive him. Maybe it was stupid, maybe I was being a sucker, but no matter how hard I fought my feelings, they wouldn't go away. God wanted me to forgive him and that was difficult. Because in forgiving him, was I headed back down a road that would lead to more hurt and pain? "You are right that I do have to forgive you. That doesn't mean that I have to date you."

"But–"

"I'm not finished. Against my better judgment, I'm going to allow you to take me out on *one date*. Trust is still a big issue between you and me and until you prove to me that you're trustworthy, we can only be friends."

He let out a sigh of relief. "Thanks. I am going to show you that you can believe in me again."

"We'll see."

I ended the call with him and felt utterly confused. Why did it seem like the more I prayed; the more hectic things became? I wanted the answer to knock me upside the head and yell out "I'm the answer!" but that wasn't going to happen. How did one simple desire for love and marriage turn into an episode of the Oprah Winfrey Show? Exhausted, I lay down on my bed and whispered a last desperate plea before going to sleep, "Please God, show me the way."

Lesson 14: Always Be a Star

She tastes and sees that her gain from work [with and for God] is good; her lamp goes not out, but burns on continually through the night [of trouble, privation, or sorrow, warning away fear, doubt, and distrust]. She lays her hands to the spindle, and her hands hold the distaff. (Proverbs 31:18-19)

"I once heard the story of a famous preacher whose wife got into an altercation in a public place. Now, I won't say who and what happened because I really don't know whether or not the story is true, but it helps introduce the importance of Proverbs 31:18. 'She tastes and sees that her gain from work, with and for God, is good; her lamp goes not out, but burns on continually through the night, of trouble, privation, or sorrow, warning away fear, doubt, and distrust.' Her lamp goes not out." Lydia looked around the room and smiled at the class. We were now in the sixth week of the class, and all twelve of us had remained faithful in attending. A quick glance around the class showed women who were growing and maturing in their understanding of womanhood, and even more importantly, in their walk with Christ.

"How do you respond when the creditor calls you demanding you make a payment?" she asked rhetorically, provoking us to think. "What do you do when the rude person cuts you off in traffic? What do you say when someone cuts you in line? How do you react when everything in your life falls apart? Are you able to be the kind, patient, loving Christian that I see right now, or does your lamp go out?"

Lydia gave us a few seconds to consider her words before continuing. "We are all called by God to be lights in this world. The world is full of darkness, and we are to be lights, showing others the way to God. Our presence alone should reflect the nature of God and cause people to be drawn to Him. The problem is that many of us have electrical issues. We have shorts in our lamps. Our oil runs out. The light is on one moment and off another. The minute anything negative happens to us, our lights flicker. We struggle with anger, resentment, fear, jealousy, sadness, helplessness, and hopelessness. We feel we need to control everything, and if one thing does not go our way, our lights instantly fade to black."

Was that my issue with men? Did I need to be in control of everything including my relationships? Did that need for control make men feel suffocated and imprisoned? When I couldn't control a man, like I couldn't control Chris, did I allow my emotions to get the best of me? In business, I needed to be in control so that my company could thrive and not be taken over by unproductive forces, but relationships didn't require that level of constraint, so was I unintentionally trying to run men so that I could feel comfortable? I had seen and heard of women who were too controlling, but never imagined I might be one of them. The thought plagued me as I continued to listen to Lydia speak.

"But a true, Godly woman knows how to keep her lamp continually burning. Notice that previous to the verse discussing her lamp it says that 'she tastes and sees that her gain from work with and for God is good.' I think the natural inclination is to separate the two parts of the verse, but that is a mistake. The verse is one. It is one verse and only one sentence. The two parts of the verse are separated by a semicolon. A semicolon is typically used when there are two different sentences or ideas, but they are directly related to each other, so instead of having them separated by a period, they are joined by a semicolon. Therefore, her lamp going not out is directly connected to her understanding her gain from work being good.

"Do you know what keeps us from handling a situation the wrong way? Experience. If we have done it either right or wrong before or witnessed it being done before, the lesson in the experience helps us to do it correctly the next time we are faced with the situation. If I am broke and don't know how the rent is going to be paid, and I get nervous and act crazy, but then at the last minute provision is made by

God and the rent is paid, that experience has taught me that God is faithful. Yes, the next time I may get nervous again, but I also may be reminded of my last experience and choose to be cool and trust God. This time I may not go off on my husband for not making enough money or on the property manager for posting an eviction notice. This time I may continually let my light shine.

"The first part of verse eighteen says that her experience has shown her that working with and for God, doing the right thing, trusting Him, and living for Him has resulted in good gain, positive results, desirable outcomes. Because of her experience she knows that she doesn't have to flip out every time something stressful comes her way. Her lamp continually burns on. When the bills are due she says, 'God, I trust you.' When they tell her that her child might be ADD or autistic she says, 'God, I know your plan is perfect.' When her husband dies she says, 'God, I know you are with me.' Her lamp burns on. There is no temporary outage of electricity or shortage of oil. Her experience has taught her that God is still in control and that there is no need to become upset or be afraid. Just keep shining and be like a bright star in the midst of a dark night."

I nodded my head in agreement. In business, I'd learned early on to learn from my mistakes and the mistakes of others. I saw too many entrepreneurs go belly-up because they kept hitting their heads against the same brick wall. I quickly understood that if you made an error, correct it if possible, and be sure to avoid doing the same thing again. Now I saw that I needed to apply this same rationale to matters of the heart. My experience shouldn't cause me to be emotional and fearful; instead it should allow me to understand what areas of my life required tweaking so that I could be better at it the next time around. I got the message: God wasn't trying to hold me back; He was trying to make me better.

"Verse nineteen reads, 'She lays her hands to the spindle, and her hands hold the distaff.' The spindle and distaff are associated with the process of sewing. She is an expert at sewing; she knows how to handle sewing equipment professionally and skillfully. Now, this story is not encouraging you to go out and take sewing lessons.

No, it is about being skillful, professional, and intentional. This woman has taken the time to learn the right way to do a task. In the same way, we should be skillful.

"Learn how to do things with excellence instead of just saying, 'Well, I did my best.' Practice, get training, and study what you don't know. At one time, I didn't know how to garden, but I watched others do it, I read the directions, and I asked for advice from folks who knew how to garden. Then I kept trying and planting and building until I was able to grow a full garden with flowers, vegetables, and herbs. Now I grow a garden every year, and my family saves money on vegetables because we grow our own. You don't have to have a green thumb, but whatever you decide to do, do it with skill and expertise."

I went home that night excited about what I'd learned in class. I now comprehended that all of my experiences, good and bad, were developing me into a woman fit to be a good wife. The example of the virtuous woman seemed to be an extremely high standard, and it was rightly so. Proverbs 31:10 asked who could find a virtuous woman, and now I understood why. Being a woman of virtue was not something one just woke up on day and became. It required commitment to God, her family, her community, and herself. I resolved that I would challenge myself to exhibit these traits in my life. The way my social calendar was looking, I would be married before I knew what hit me. If I was going to take that next step, I wanted to be a wife of extreme value, one who epitomized womanhood. No longer would I question whether or not I was good enough to have the love of a good man. I just wondered who the lucky guy would be who would win my heart and hand.

Lesson 15: Listen More Than You Speak

A [self-confident] fool's lips bring contention, and his mouth invites a beating. A [self-confident] fool's mouth is his ruin, and his lips are a snare to himself.

(Proverbs 18:6-7)

Wednesday morning, Gold, Perkins, and I had our first meeting with the Green Global executives since the Savannah dinner cruise. Their lawyers had responded to the contractual issues we had addressed and offered some compromises, but we still were not completely satisfied with the deal. I sat back during the meeting and watched as Perkins and Gold informed the group of our pending concerns, which was a first for me. I noticed Perkins kept peeking at me, probably waiting for me to cut Gold off and offer my perspective. Once, when I caught him gawking, I actually winked at him and nodded as if to say, "You're doing a great job. Keep up the good work!" He lowered his head and frowned, astonished by my one hundred and eighty degree change of attitude.

Gold, on the other hand, was in his element. He hardly noticed that I wasn't fighting with him for control. He was too busy using big words like conglomerates and enjoying the sound of his own voice to notice me at all. Instead of my usual banter, I inconspicuously scrutinized the mannerisms of the Green Global execs. I studied the way they answered questions, the glances they gave to one another, the nonverbal behavior that was typically overlooked. Interestingly enough, I didn't like what I saw. I could tell by their conduct that not only did they think they were superior to us, but they didn't intend to give us the best negotiation. In my six months on working on this venture, I had never noticed their arrogance before, quite possibly because I was too busy cat fighting with Gold to see the truth staring me in the face.

After our meeting, Perkins, Gold, and I had lunch to discuss our impressions of the conference with Green Global. Gold kept rubbing my hand and shoulder throughout lunch, eventually causing Perkins to lose all couth and blurt out, "Okay, what in the world is going on with you two?"

"I beg your pardon?" I asked scrupulously, wanting to keep him at bay a little longer.

His face reddened. "Come on now! I'm no fool. Ross, you went the entire meeting without saying more than a dozen words and without once combating anything Gold said. Now, Gold is over here looking at you with puppy dog eyes, as if he just found a brand new bone."

Gold and I gazed at each other and broke into laughter. Perkins was clearly onto us and not taking anything less than the truth. I reached across the table and grabbed Perkins' hand, enclosing it with mine. "We're not trying to upset you. I just decided to let Gold handle things today. Aren't you the one always telling me to be professional and stop arguing with him?"

"Yes, but you never listened! What's changed?" he questioned as he pulled his hand away from me and lifted his water glass to his mouth to drink.

I smirked. "I've changed. I'm becoming a better woman, and Gold's changed too. Right, Gold?"

Gold grinned proudly. "Yes. I am loving the new and improved Ross. In fact, I'm loving her so much that I'm going to make her Mrs. Gold one of these days."

Perkins choked on his water. We had to pat him on his back a few times before he was able to catch his breath. For a moment, I thought we were going to have to call an EMS.

Eyes red from gagging, Perkins glared at us in disbelief. "Ross and Gold a couple? That's comedy! You guys can barely get along for five minutes."

"We've been together for hours today without any strife," I challenged.

Perkins scratched his salt and pepper colored beard. "Mmm. You're right. So when did this all happen? How did this all happen?"

I put my hand up in defense. "Long story, but don't jump to any conclusions. We are just getting to know each other. Nothing's set in stone."

"Don't listen to her," Gold objected. "I know Ross is trying to play the conservative role, but this is a match made in heaven. It won't be long before you're buying us a wedding present."

"Of all of the unusual things in this world, I never would have thought...I would have bet on cows flying before I guessed you two would hook up!" Perkins hooted.

"Me too," I offered, "but stranger things have happened. Not to change the subject, but since I wasn't quarreling with Gold, I actually got the chance to observe the GG execs, and to tell you the truth, I'm really not sure about this thing anymore."

Both Gold and Perkins glowered at me. This was not the feedback they were looking for from me. Perkins was the first to probe for more information. "What exactly concerns you, and why didn't you say anything at the meeting?"

Sighing, I searched for a way to explain my feelings to them. "Well, I wanted to gather more concrete evidence before I ruined our rapport with them. Right now, it's just a hunch. There was something distrustful about the way they dealt with us today. I honestly don't believe they will be fair with us in the end."

Gold read the expression on Perkins' face and decided to play the buffer. "Ross, why don't you look more into what you're sensing, and if you find any valid proof we can address it. Until then, let's continue with business as planned."

Perkins and I nodded in agreement, but I could tell that I had just crossed the line and was now entering enemy territory. The last thing any businessperson wants to hear is that he has just wasted six months of time and money on a bad deal.

"I'm going to get another beer. Do you want anything else?" Chris asked me that Friday night as we feasted on wings and fries at a local sports bar.

I winced. "No, I'm good." He turned away from the table and disappeared into the crowd. He'd already consumed four beers; this would be his fifth. Although he didn't seem to be intoxicated and was handling the alcohol quite well, I still felt uneasy. The last thing I wanted to deal with was a drunken date. I hoped he didn't think that if he got hammered that he was going home with me. That was out of the question. I would call a taxi and pay the cabbie fifty bucks to drive him back to Jonesboro before I'd let him waddle his way into my car.

Despite his excess of drinks, so far the date was going fairly decent. We had spent the past two hours reminiscing about the good times in our relationship. Like the time we went to the Movie in the Park at Centennial Park and got soaking wet from running to the car in the rain. Or when we visited his coworker's church and realized thirty minutes into the service that it was a cult and had to lie our way out the door. Or the time we went to the Georgia Aquarium, starring at the wondrous sea life, captivated by the glory of God.

I enjoyed hanging out with Chris, and I still cared about him, but I couldn't seem to shake this nagging feeling like it was time to let him go. He had spent so much time during our dating thanking me for giving him another chance that I felt bad that I was thinking so negatively. The fact that I had other men in my life also didn't help. For the first time in a long time, I didn't feel so desperate and lonely. Maybe my new sense of peace had nothing to do with the men in my life and more to do with my growing relationship with the Lord.

"Did you miss me?" Chris inquired as he returned and thumped his new bottle of beer on the table.

I shot him an unenthusiastic smile and changed the subject. "So, how's work?"

"Ah, work's fine, work's good, work's work. Same thing, different day. My supervisor's been riding me lately, but what's new?" He tossed his head back and guzzled the beer as if it were a hot day and he was parched. I shook my head, wondering when he started drinking this way. I had seen him have a beer or two in the past, but never chain drink. Something was seriously off.

"I don't remember you drinking so much," I said, trying to approach the subject lightly.

He waved my comment away. "Oh, you know. Just a few beers, not really a big deal."

"Mmm. I guess not. Chris, I've had a great time tonight, but I really need to head home. It's been a busy week, and I'm drained." Avoiding eye contact, I gathered my purse and jacket.

"Awe! Already? The night is still young. Come on, Amber. We could catch a movie or something. You remember when we used to go to the midnight show? We can go tonight."

"As much as that's a tempting offer, I think I'd better go." I didn't want to hurt his feelings, but I wasn't about to sit around and watch him get wasted. He was hiding something. I knew him well enough to know that. I would try to deal with whatever it was when he was sober, but talking about it now would be a waste of time. "Are you going to be okay? How are you going to get home?"

"Yeah, yeah, I'm good. Don't worry about me. I'll probably stay and watch the game. Lakers versus the Heat."

I nodded and kissed him on the forehead. "Okay, goodnight."

As I walked out of the bar, I turned back and peered into the establishment's window. There was Chris, at the bar, ordering another beer. *Lord, what is he doing? Please protect him.*

That night I really prayed. Not a few words lackadaisically directed at God like I'd been doing for years, but a get-down-on-my-knees-and-seek-Him-wholeheartedly prayer. There was so much going on in my life that required His guidance and His intervention. For the first time, I realized that I was relying too heavily on my own understanding to handle the issues in my life. I wasn't taking the time to have a conversation with God; a dialogue where he could speak back to me and address my presented concerns.

I might not have received the answers I needed that night, but I did feel the sort of peace that only comes from heaven, the kind that surpasses understanding. I knew that God would cover Chris and whatever he was going through. I was certain that He would reveal the true spirit behind the Green Global deal. I believed that whatever man was meant for me would prove himself faithful in time. My life was all in His hands, the big things, the little things, and my heart.

Lesson 16: Cover Up!

She opens her hand to the poor, yes, she reaches out her filled hands to the needy [whether in body, mind, or spirit]. She fears not the snow for her family, for all her household are doubly clothed in scarlet. (Proverbs 31:20-21)

"Some of us will never be like the virtuous woman because we don't know how to give. We want to decide what to give, when to give it, and whom to give it to. Proverbs 31:20 says, 'She opens her hand to the poor, yes, she reaches out her filled hands to the needy, whether in body, mind or spirit.'" Lydia sat on the desk in the front of the room and kicked off her shoes, leaving her stocking covered feet exposed.

"Okay, so maybe you worked at the soup kitchen last Thanksgiving or gave some clothes to Goodwill, or even gave that beggar at the intersection a dollar, but is that really enough?"

No one dared to respond. It was the seventh class, and we were now familiar with her teaching style. She knew how to deliver the Word in a way that made us realize that all of our righteousness was like the bible said, "as filthy rags." We figured the gut punch was coming right about…now.

"Many people would think it is enough. 'Hey, I've done my part,' they boast. However, truly, they've done nothing at all. They have barely scratched the surface."

See what I meant? I knew that she was far from done.

"What about when a family member or friend comes to you and says, 'My lights are getting cut off' or 'I'm being evicted,' how do you respond? What happens when people show up at your house hungry? What about when you see a need in your community going undone? When you hear about that family down the street with six children who don't have decent shoes or enough to eat?"

I was getting the point which was causing me to feel guilty. Did I give enough to others in my family or community? Probably not. *Thanks a lot, Lydia!*

"Church folks think they are really doing something because we give our ten percent tithes and a little extra for offering at church." She scanned the faces of the women in the room and quickly added, "Now, I am not suggesting anything as it relates to your tithes or offering, so calm down. What I am saying is that there is a real need all around us, 24 hours 7 days a week, 365 days a year, and often we ignore it because we think that if we have given tithes and offering in church then we have done our parts. However, we are deceiving ourselves.

"Verse twenty doesn't say she gives to the poor once a year when she cleans out her closet or on Christmas. It doesn't say she gives a few dollars to her church and hopes they will handle feeding the poor in her neighborhood. It says that she opens and reaches out her filled hands to the poor and needy. She is the one organizing the clothing drive. She is the one going down to the soup kitchen once a month or even once a week. She is inviting people into her home, feeding them, and sending them away with a plate. She is scraping up some money to help pay a light bill or water bill…and wait! She gives than says, 'Don't worry about paying me back.' She drives that mother down from the street to the welfare office or to a charity to get help to find shoes for those six kids. Giving is not a one-time thing. Giving is not complacent. Giving is not passive. Giving is active, aggressive, ongoing, and intentional."

Lydia got down from the table and walked around the classroom, still shoeless. "But she takes it a step further. The needy are not just those who are monetarily poor. There are needy people sitting in this room today. There are needy rich people. Neediness is not just physical or bodily. Someone can be spiritually or mentally needy, spiritually or mentally poor. The reason I am teaching this course, a 13-week course, and not getting paid a dime to do it is because there are mentally and spiritually poor women who need this information. There is more than one way to give to people and more than one population that needs your gifts. People need your prayers, your encouragement, your testimonies, your support, your wisdom, and your knowledge. Give with filled hands. Give from your abundance. That's how a virtuous woman gives."

I considered myself somewhat of a giver. I donated money and clothing periodically to various causes, and annually I gave my employees bonuses at Christmas, but I knew there was a lot more I could be doing. Like my younger brother was married with two kids. I knew he needed help financially, but I was still holding a grudge with him for dropping out of college to get married. Or my mother; I tried to help her out from time to time, but I was so afraid that she was going to squander my money on Otis, I limited the amount of help I offered. I had also considered offering some free business workshops to women in the community, but I was so busy building my empire, I didn't have the time to put something like that together.

I felt the Holy Spirit leading me to take the time to reevaluate my priorities. If I wanted to be married and be a good wife, I couldn't continue to pour all of my time and energy into my businesses. Something would have to give. As much as I hated to admit it, the old adage was right: you can't have it all. You can have a lot, and even most of it, but trying to have it all at once was like trying to be God, and that just wasn't possible. I could have a successful career and I could have a family, but I would have to make sacrifices. I just needed to choose what sacrifices I could and couldn't live with.

Lydia went back to the desk and eased up onto its surface again. "I am sure that most of you are familiar with the significance of the Passover. Just in case anyone here is not, I will briefly explain it. When Moses was sent by God to tell Pharaoh to let the children of Israel go, Pharaoh refused. One of the consequences of his refusal was that an angel of death came through Egypt, killing all of the firstborns. However, God's people were 'passed over' because they had the front door posts of their houses marked with lamb's blood. To mark the door posts, they took a wool called scarlet and soaked it in a mixture of blood, water, and hyssop, and wiped it along the two sides of the door post and the top.

"That being said, verse twenty one states, 'She fears not the snow for her family, for all of her household are doubly clothed in scarlet.' There is another story in the Book of Joshua about a woman named Rahab who hid two of the Israeli spies. Because of her faith and actions, when Jericho was defeated by the Israelites, she and her family were spared. She was told to hang a scarlet cord from her window as a sign that her family was to be saved.

"These are two different biblical incidents in which scarlet was used to save families from death. Therefore, in verse twenty-one we can now understand the significance of what is being said. She is not afraid of the snow or difficulties because her family is protected. They are not just somewhat protected, they are doubly protected, double clothed in scarlet.

"This woman had prepared her family for hardships that threatened their lives. Like the Israelites, she followed God's instructions and covered her family in the blood of the Lamb. She knew that when death and destruction came near, it would pass over her home because they were covered by the blood of Jesus."

"Amen," a sister in the back of the room yelled out.

Lydia nodded in agreement. "Ladies, we have to start covering up. We have to prepare our families for the rainy days by covering them spiritually, mentally, and physically. If I send my child outside in January without a coat or jacket, the Department of Family and Children Services is going to come to my house and tell me that I am neglecting my child because I haven't prepared him for the harsh weather. That child needs to be covered and protected from the cold. In the same manner, we have to cover our entire family, dipping them twice in the blood of Jesus."

When I walked into my house that evening, I felt spiritually full as if I had just eaten a seven course meal. I looked around the living room of my four bedroom with four bathrooms home and was instantly reminded of what I needed to do. Immediately, I promised myself that I would not go on anymore dates that week. I loved all the attention from Chris, Gold, and Eric, but I just needed some quiet time to sort other areas of my life out. If I were planning to eventually commit myself to a man, I would first have to commit myself to being a better me.

Lesson 17: Count the Costs

But he who did not know and did things worthy of a beating shall be beaten with few [lashes]. For everyone to whom much is given, of him shall much be required; and of him to whom men entrust much, they will require and demand all the more.

(Luke 12:48)

Instead of spending the rest of the week at my office, I called Eric to let him know that I would be checking up on the other businesses and asked him to forward my calls to my cell phone. I rarely spent any time at the daycare or bakery, and it was time that I stopped in and made sure everything was running smoothly.

To be real, I wanted an opportunity to review the things in my life that were important to me, starting with my businesses. I also wanted to spend some time at home, away from the hum and drum of the world in order to put some issues in my life in perspective. Except for the time I spent sleeping, my house was absent of my presence. I had paid $300K for a house that I had yet to use all of the bathrooms.

On Tuesday, I hung out at Sweet Tooth Oasis, talking to the manager and employees and getting a feel of its daily operations. On Wednesday, I visited Sunrise Sunset Daycare, monitoring the staff and children; seeing what was working and what was not. On Thursday and Friday, I stayed home and cleaned my entire house from to bottom for the first time since I had moved into it.

Cleaning gave me time to mull over the various thoughts racing through my mind. The last Wife 101 class on giving had me thinking about how many resources I had that I wasn't sharing with others. I didn't view myself as stingy, but I had been so focused on building myself up that I had never stopped and considered what I could do with what I already had. I guess I was waiting to get all of my ducks in a row before I reached out and did more, but like Lydia suggested, I could do so much in my community right now. So much needed to be done, but where should I start?

"God, show me what I can do for others; how you want me to give. And help me to be obedient, no matter what the cost."

I wasn't sure what God had in mind for me to do. I had a few ideas, but I wanted to wait until I heard directly from Him before I moved. Lately it seemed that heaven was a bit silent. I had been praying about a lot of things including Gold, Chris, and Eric, but God's will for me still wasn't clear. Maybe I wasn't listening closely. Maybe I just needed to be still and let God reveal his plans to me.

While at home, I also decided to do a little investigating. The Green Global deal was still not sitting well with me. I made a few phone calls to some people I knew who "know people." My people said they would do some digging and get back to me when they had something solid. Sounded like something from a mafia movie, didn't it?

By Saturday, I was itching to get out. I wanted to learn how to spend more time at home, but I would have to do so slowly. Hey, Rome wasn't built in one day!

Typical me, I called good old Tisha and invited her to hit the mall with me. By 3:00 p.m., we were walking through Perimeter Mall with shopping bags from The Limited, Bebe, Victoria's Secret, Nordstrom's, and Bloomingdale's. Makeup next on the agenda, we scurried into M.A.C. and, of course, Tisha got suckered into a complimentary makeover. As the makeup artist dabbed foundation on her face, I leaned against the counter and told her about my week.

"Can you believe I haven't been to my office since Monday? I mean, yes, I've been working, but you know how I feel about my office. It's like my throne!"

Tisha let out a faint giggle, trying not to interfere with the makeup application. "Yeah, that's so not like you. Hmm. I wish I could just take the week off wherever I felt like it."

"I didn't take the week off. I spent Tuesday and Wednesday at the other companies, and I took off only Thursday and Friday, for your information."

"Oh, okay I stand corrected. I wish I could just take off Thursday and Friday wherever I felt like it."

"That sounds better." I chuckled. "I actually cleaned my house. It wasn't bad because Karen the housekeeper comes twice a month, but I think I could do the whole domestic thing again. I still love the smell of bleach mixed with elbow grease."

"You and that bleach! I remember back at Emory when we almost passed out because you poured a bottle of bleach all over our dorm room floor!"

"That floor was nasty! I wasn't about to jump down off my bed at night and step onto that crusty tile. It needed to be disinfected! No telling what the previous occupants had done on that floor before we moved in," I cackled. "But seriously, you know when I was at the daycare, I started thinking that maybe we should start offering free parenting classes. Some of those moms send their kids to Sunrise looking like a hot mess. When I talked to the staff, they said that many of the kids come from single parent households and the mothers really don't have a clue on how to rear their children."

Tisha closed her eyes as the woman applied eye shadow and liner. "It's a good idea, but how are you going to get the parents to come? Those folks don't want anyone telling them how to raise their children."

"I considered that. Then I was thinking we could offer some kind of incentive like a $100 gift card for school clothes for every parent who successfully completed the class, something that will benefit both the parent and the child. I just feel like I need to do more. I have this facility, and yes, we're helping them with childcare, but we could do a lot more than that. I've been also thinking that I want to offer free business seminars to women through the real estate office."

"When did you get all Mother Teresa on me?"

"I know, right! Girl, it's this class I'm taking. It's really making me change my thinking. I actually had the idea for the women's business class for a while, but it seemed like I didn't have the time. Now, I see that if I rearranged my priorities, I could do more for others. I'm tired of everything being all about me."

"You're on your own with that idea because I'll never get tired of having everything be all about me! If you don't think about you, who will?" Tisha opened her eyes and stiffened her lips as the woman coated her lips with M.A.C.'s lip glass.

"God will. If we stop worrying so much about ourselves, we will finally see that God is able to handle anything we throw at Him."

"Okay, I know you've been spending way too much time at that church. You're starting to sound all religious."

"Oh, I'm not being religious; I'm being real," I said with a hint of attitude.

The makeup artist handed Tisha a mirror and walked away to help another customer. Tisha gawked at herself in the mirror, clearly impressed by her new look. "Well Miss Real, what's really going on with the fellas? Did you cut Eric off yet? And please tell me that you finally called Chris back."

"Yes, I talked to Chris. We actually went out last week. No, I haven't cut Eric off. He's a really nice guy, and I don't want to be too hasty."

Tisha rolled her eyes. "Hasty? Anyway, what's going on with Chris? How was the date?"

I sighed. "It was good, but he had a few too many beers. He wasn't inebriated or anything, but something wasn't right about him. It almost seemed like he was trying to drink away his problems. I think there may be more to the whole Noel thing than he is letting on. How do you go from being super in love and getting married to absolutely nothing? It's doesn't make sense, and now he's dying to be back with me? I saw the way he looked at her at that engagement party, and he has never, ever looked at me like that."

Tisha placed the mirror down on the counter and turned towards me. "Yeah, it doesn't add up. But the way I see it, you have two choices. Work things out with Chris and forget about what happened in the past, or forget Chris and let Gold pay your bills. Eric isn't even an option. Hey, that's just my opinion. Do what you want with it."

I got home from shopping that evening around 6 o'clock. I walked through the front door, tossed my keys and purse onto the console in the foyer, and pressed play on my answering machine, my usual routine. Gold, Chris, and Eric had all called. Not surprising. Delete. I had a few other calls from telemarketers or somebody trying to get me to do something I didn't want to do. Delete. The last message, however, was so unexpected that I had to play it twice.

"Amber, this is your brother, Alex. Uh, got some bad news. Mom and Dad's house caught on fire about a week ago. They're okay and no one was hurt, but now they don't have anywhere to live while the insurance company rebuilds the house. They've been staying at my place, but you know that with me, Gina, and the kids, we already have a cramped apartment. I know it's an inconvenience, but I was wondering if you could at least send them a little money so they could get a hotel room in the meantime. You know I wouldn't ask unless it was an emergency. Call me back and let me know if you can help."

I began to pace the length of my foyer, Alex's words replaying through my mind. Fire about a week ago. *Why was I just hearing about this now?* They're okay, and no one was hurt. Don't have anywhere to live. Send them a little money.

I covered my face with my hands in distress. Earlier today I had prayed and asked God what he wanted me to do, and now the answer had come as bold and powerful as lightening. How could I not help my mom? What kind of daughter would I be? Although I didn't care much for Otis, I couldn't help her and not help him. They were a package deal, and I would have to suck up my pride and do the right thing, despite the cost to my emotions.

Taking a deep breath in then exhaling, I picked up the cordless, house phone and called my brother back. He answered on the third ring.

"Alex? It's Amber. I got your message."

"Hey. I'm glad you called back so quickly. I know you stay busy."

"Yeah, well, I took a few days off. So, how's mom?"

"She's okay. I'll let you talk to her yourself. Hold on."

"Hello?"

"Hi, Mom. It's Amber."

"Hey honey! How are you?"

"I'm good, Mom. Alex told me what happened with the house. Why didn't you call me?"

"We're okay. Don't you worry. I know you are busy, and I didn't want to disturb you. The insurance company is going to take care of everything."

"Mom, I'm never too busy for something like this. You know you can't stay with Alex. There's not enough room over there."

"I know, honey. We were going to try to find a cheap hotel since we might have to be there for a while."

"Nonsense. I will send you and Otis plane tickets and you guys can come and stay at my house as long as you need."

"You would let us stay with you?"

"Of course, Mom. I'm sorry that you thought I wouldn't. I'm hardly ever home anyway so at least you can enjoy my house since I'm not."

"Oh, praise God! Thank you, honey! We'll stay out of your way."

"Mom, my house is your house. You won't be in my way. I'll book your tickets tonight and call you back with the itinerary. Okay?"

"Are you sure?"

"I'm sure."

I lied. I wasn't sure.

Lesson 18: Behind Every Great Man is a Virtuous Woman

She makes for herself coverlets, cushions, and rugs of tapestry. Her clothing is of linen, pure and fine, and of purple [such as that of which the clothing of the priest and the hallowed clothes of the temple were made]. Her husband is known in the [city's] gates, when he sits among the elders of the land. (Proverbs 31:22-23)

It was all settled. Mom and Otis were coming in on a flight on Tuesday evening. I had mixed feelings about their stay, but it was too late to dwell on my reneging emotions now. It was going to take at least another four to six months to repair the damages to their house, meaning that I would have to parent-sit until late summer/early fall. It had been over five years since I'd spent any significant amount of time around them, so I wasn't sure how we would all get along. The good thing was that with my busy schedule, I would probably only see them at night and a little on the weekends.

I had them set up to camp out in the guest suite which was on the opposite end of the hallway from my room (on purpose, of course!). I had also rented them a 4-door sedan with my corporate account so I wouldn't have to worry about chauffeuring them around or them messing up my Mustang (Hands off my baby!). I'd filled the cabinets and fridge with groceries so they could cook what they wanted. Taking care of their immediate needs in advance would keep them out of my hair at least for the first week or two. I hoped.

I was praying that something Lydia said at our next class on Monday would help me cope better with the idea of living with Mom and Otis again. I loved them, but old childhood resentments were still unresolved and would more than likely quickly resurface. Just the thought of Otis trying to regulate my mom or run something in my house made me straight loco. Moreover, he better not spill anything on my carpet! *Ooh, Lord Jesus, please help me!*

The moment I entered class, a sense of peace came upon me. As always, Lydia's teachings helped put me back in a spirit-led frame of mind.

"Proverbs 31:22 reads, 'She makes for herself coverlets, cushions, and rugs of tapestry. Her clothing is of linen, pure and fine, and of purple, such as that of which the clothing of the priest and hollowed clothes of the temple were made.' This is the first and only time in this chapter that it discusses something that she does only for herself and not for others. Every other verse from Proverbs 31:10-31 is about who she is and what she does as it relates to others.

"The twenty-second verse reveals two very important things about this woman. First, it shows that she is a selfless person. She is not like many of us who spend our entire days focused on ourselves. She is not sitting around complaining about how poorly people treat her and how she isn't going to do anything for others anymore. She is not asking her husband that old Janet Jackson question, 'What have you done for me lately?' He favorite people are not Me, Myself, and I. No, not this woman. Her focus is on God and others. The fact that only one verse discusses her energy spent on herself allows us to conclude that she understands that love is not self-seeking."

Lydia cleared her throat and continued. "Second, this verse demonstrates quality self-care. Although she is not self-absorbed, she also does not neglect herself. She values herself as a woman and treats herself with love and care. Her clothing is pure and fine and the color worn by highly regarded people. Often when we see selfless women, their level of self-care is lacking. Everyone else has on nice clothes, but they haven't brought a new dress for themselves in years. They are giving away new shoes, but new shoes have not graced their feet in months. They will do someone else's child's hair all fancy and pretty, but they haven't seen the inside of a beauty salon in a decade. A lack of self-care is not synonymous with godliness.

"Ladies, in the process of loving others and giving of yourselves, remember to love yourselves too. You deserve a 'me' day from time to time. It's okay to buy a new dress, get a pedicure, and splurge a little on a pair of those shoes you've been eyeing. The problem is not taking care of yourself or doing something nice for yourself. No, it occurs when your focus shifts to you, 24-7. It's when you think about nothing but you. It's when you're buying up the mall at the expense of bills that need to be paid. It's when you have to work two and three jobs to afford to shoe shop every week. Love yourself enough to treat yourself like royalty; however, love God enough to live with the mentality that it's not all about you, but about Him."

Lydia picked up a bottle of water from the desk near her, took a sip, and then placed it back on the desk. "You know, and this is slightly off topic but still relevant, one of the reasons it is important not to be self-focused is because that is usually the vehicle the enemy uses to keep you trapped in negative emotions. When you are looking at yourself, you begin to notice everything that is wrong, everything that is missing, everything that is unfair. You start to feel depressed; you start to complain. All the things you think you should have but don't seem to consume your thoughts. Your peace evaporates; your joy dissolves. You are no longer receptive to the still, small voice of God because you've got self-pity, resentment, anger, depression, and every other negative thought and feeling yelling so loudly at you.

"At this point, how can you truly be of use to God? You're in a downward spiral and the only way to get out is to refocus back on the Lord. You don't have all the answers, but He does. You can't control many of the issues of your life, but He can. Selflessness keeps you focused on the big picture and from being overtaken by the enemy's plan for your life: to kill, steal, and destroy you and your relationship with God. But that's a topic for a different time; let's get back to the lesson.

"Verse 23 is a unique verse, probably the most interesting verse of the chapter. 'Her husband is known in the city's gates, when he sits among the elders of the land.' What's so fascinating about this verse is its position in the chapter. At the beginning of the chapter, verses 10-12 discuss this woman as she relates to her man.

Verses 13-22 and then verses 24-31 go onto to describe the qualities about her that make her such an asset to her family and community. Verse 23, however, is oddly placed in the middle of the description of this wonderful woman, but it does not once mention any directly related to her…or so it seems."

Lydia paused, looked up at us, and grinned, satisfied that she was holding us in suspense. After a few moments, she peered back down at her bible and said, "Let's read it again. 'Her husband is known in the city's gates, when he sits among the elders of the land.' This verse is about her husband, not her. Why would the author write all of these great things about this woman, and right in the middle of it all, say something about her husband, and then go back to talking about her again? It appears as if the writer has a little Attention Deficit Disorder."

A few giggles were heard around the room.

"Despite its awkwardness, I don't believe this verse is out of place at all. It is just as much about the virtuous woman as the other verses in this chapter. It is right, smack-dab in the middle so that the reader won't get the wrong impression and think the verse is about her husband rather than her. If the verse was at the beginning or end, we would naturally want to believe it was about the man in her life, but because it is in the middle, we have to understand that this verse reflects her, not him.

"He is known when he sits among the elders. He is known because of her. She is such an amazing woman that her virtue catapults him into celebrity status. Most great men are who they are because of the great women in their lives. Their success in the world is directly linked to our success as wives and mothers. For this reason, most elevated positions such as pastors, bishops, presidents, and other leaders, in order to be elected or appointed men are often required to be married. A good wife does more than just looks good on a man's arm; she thrusts him into his purpose. When you see a man who is living beneath his potential, often you also see a woman who is not exuding virtue. Now, I am not blaming women for the shortcomings of men, but if a woman is not in her position and filling her role, how can a man be in his position and fulfilling his role? Everyone has to do their part. If the left leg moves outward, but the right leg doesn't do anything, you cannot walk. You need both legs participating in collaboration to walk. In the same manner, men and women have to collaborate for the sake of family success."

I mentally chewed on the week's lesson as if it was a tender, succulent steak. Point one: take care of myself but don't be self-focused. Point two: the success of the man in my life is directly linked to me. I was amazed that Lydia was able to pull from the scriptures these profound messages that I had never considered when reading the verses in the past. In a weird way, I felt like God was answering my questions about my disappointing love life. Had I been married in the past, I would have probably ruined the married with a bunch of backward thinking and my "take no prisoners" attitude. If I wanted not only to attract a good man, but also to keep him, I would have to keep working on my inner beauty, not just my resume. I was now figuring out that the most wonderful and beautiful thing about me was the Christ in me and that discovery would be from which I would draw my future husband to me, if it hadn't already.

I resolved with my mind to have a positive outlook on my new house guests. Maybe having them live with me for a while was a test from God to see if I could be selfless, if I could put the needs of others before my own. If I were going to have a family of my own, I would most certainly need to demonstrate this characteristic. I also decided to continue to proceed slowly with Gold, Chris, and Eric. Whichever guy was for me, if any of them, would be clear and apparent in time. In the meantime, I would just keep on letting them battle it out for my heart.

Being the center of attention is hard work, but somebody has got to do it!

Lesson 19: There's No Place Like Home

Seek, inquire for, and require the Lord while He may be found [claiming Him by necessity and by right]; call upon Him while he is near. Let the wicked forsake his way and the unrighteous man his thoughts; and let him return to the Lord, and He will have love, pity, and mercy for him, and to our God, for He will multiply to him His abundant pardon. For My thoughts are not your thoughts, neither are your ways My ways, says the Lord. (Isaiah 55:6-8)

By the time I took my ninth deep breath, Eric started to look very concerned. "Are you okay, Boss?" he asked while placing his hand on my shoulder in comfort.

We stood at the rear end of the baggage claim area of Hartsfield-Jackson Airport, just above the escalators that welcomed arriving passengers to the city of Hotlanta. Any moment now, my mom and Otis would ascend from the escalator and become instant residences of my household. I thought I could handle the responsibility, but with reality staring me in the face, I realized I was weaker than I wanted to be.

I took another deep breath in and exhaled. "Yeah. It's just a little more nerve wrecking than I thought it would be."

Tuesday morning I woke up in a tizzy. I tried ineffectively throughout the day to slow down the erratic beating of my heart, but it was useless. What in the world was I thinking, telling them they could stay with me? For six months? I couldn't stand to be on the phone with my mother for six minutes, and now I was going to have her living with me for six months? I felt like I had signed and dated my own death certificate.

I was so much in a state of panic that Eric cornered me at the office and forced me to tell him what was eating at me. Disclosing the situation with my mom and Otis was somewhat therapeutic, but the anxiety in my chest would not recede, at least not that easily. Eric, being a caring person, offered to go with me to the airport and be my tower of strength. Thank God for Eric because without him, I might have not showed up to pick them up or worse, sent a car for them!

Another deep breath. Eric moved behind me, placing both of his hands near my collarbone and engaging me in a neck and shoulder massage. "Mmmm," I groaned, mentally thanking God again for Eric. What was wrong with me? Why wasn't I head over heels in love with this sweet man? Ladies, why do we do this? We have a nice guy in our lives, but for some reason it is just not enough. Something is always missing! For me, it was the spark, the fire, the passion. I wanted flames, and with Eric there wasn't even smoke!

Otis was the first to appear as the escalator ascended. He wore sunglasses as if he just landed at Miami's International Airport instead of Atlanta's. Three seconds later, my mother emerged several stairs behind him, dressed in northern winter apparel, a thick wool coat, crocheted hat, and snow boots. "That's them," I whispered to Eric who immediately stopped rubbing my shoulders and approached them to help them with their carry-on luggage.

I pasted on the biggest smile I could muster up and stepped towards the older couple. "Hi! You guys made it."

My mother reached out for me, and I allowed her to pull me in for a tight, 10-second, sway from side-to-side hug. "Look at my baby! Otis, look at my beautiful baby!"

Embarrassed and feeling like I'd regressed into a little girl, I blushed and pulled away from her arms. "I'd like you to meet a friend of mine, Eric. Eric, this is my mom, Anita, and her husband, Otis."

Eric and Otis shook hands and mumbled greetings. My mother scanned Eric from head to toe then glanced at me with an inquisitive grin. I knew what she was thinking, that Eric was my man, but he wasn't. I would have to correct her later on…in private…away from Eric's sensitive ears.

"It's good to meet you, sweetie!" my mother exclaimed before pulling Eric into a tight hug.

I shook my head in slight annoyance. From the early age of fifteen, my mother had been trying to figure out what boys I dated, which guys I liked, and what man would become my husband. She would bring different young men to me in attempts to "hook us up," telling me that a young woman should start a family soon after high school. My mother never seemed to value getting an education or having a career. She couldn't understand why a woman would forego family life for independence and career satisfaction. Looking back now, I wished I would have been a little more balanced about my career and family life ideas. Maybe my way wasn't the way, but neither was hers. A mixture of both ideas was the happy medium that would have given me the life I truly wanted.

I knew if I didn't quickly change the subject, my mom would have been talking about future grandchildren with Eric, so I quickly intervened. "Mom, let's go see if your luggage is on the conveyer belt, and you can tell us about your flight during the drive home."

Two hours later, I had sent Eric home, and my mom and Otis were settled into their room for the night. I made myself a caramel cappuccino, still trying to wrap my brain around my feelings towards my house guests. Leaning back on the brown leather sofa, I inhaled the rich aroma of the drink, permitting the steam to warm my face. I closed my eyes and took a sip of the hot liquid. It felt good to zone-out, forgetting all of the worries in my life and simply concentrate on that moment.

"Hmm mm," the sound of a throat clearing startled me. I looked up to see my mother standing over me, smiling and wearing an oversize nightgown and men's house shoes. "Amber, I really appreciate you letting us stay here. This is such a beautiful home! That suite you got us in is better than staying at the Marriott! And the rental car? I never wanted you to go out of your way for us, but we really, really appreciate what you've done."

I placed the mug on the coffee table in front of me. "It's no problem, Mom. We're family, and you needed help."

Mom plopped down on the sofa next to me. "I am so proud of you. I knew you were doing well down here, but it is something else to see it with my own two eyes. God is good all the time, and all the time, God is good!"

"Yes, He is." I hated clichés, but what else was I supposed to say?

"So you know I am dying to ask. Is Eric your guy friend?" Her smile turned from sincere to meddlesome.

"No, Mom. Eric is actually an employee of mine. He's the office manager for the realty."

She poked out her bottom lip. "What? You got that good looking man working for you, and you haven't snapped him up? And he is so nice and honorable. Got good home training. You need a husband like him. And babies too! What are you waiting for? The Rapture?"

"I'm not waiting for anything. He does like me, but there just isn't any chemistry between us." I truly did not want to talk about Eric with my mom. She and I didn't have that kind of relationship where I could be completely honest with my feelings about men. I knew that she would try to get me to see things from her viewpoint instead of letting me do it my own way.

She frowned. "Chemistry? Hm. If you don't have chemistry with him, who do you got it with?"

"There are a couple other guys I've been seeing." I knew I shouldn't have said that, but I just couldn't help myself. A small part of me loved rebelling.

She cut her eyes at me. "Amber Denise Ross." Uh oh. The full name? A lecture was sure to follow. "Now, I know you don't think I know anything about life, but your momma is not as dumb as you think. I don't know these other gentlemen you've been seeing, but the one I met tonight is worth keeping. He might not send shivers down your spine right now, but give him a chance and eventually he will. Selecting the right man is not about how nervous he makes you; it's about how much you can be you when you're with him. If he knows you, I mean even the ugly, stankin' sides of you, and still wants you, that's all the chemistry you need. Trust me, young lady, you do have some ugly and stankin' sides."

Her words penetrated me. Twenty minutes later as I sat alone in the same spot, the echo of her statement replayed in my head. Was it really that simple? Just find someone who wants you despite your flaws? Were sparks and chemistry unnecessary? Or did those feelings develop over time with the right person?

I tried to consider everyone's opinion, but it seemed that everyone had something different to say. Tisha thought I should drop Eric because he wasn't on my level. Technically, she was right. He worked for me; how could he ever stand toe to toe with me? Shouldn't I be with someone who complemented me, someone who had just as much going for them as I did? Gold seemed more suitable. He actually had way more to offer than I did, and Tisha thought he was a better fit. Gold, however, was arrogant and materialistic. Could I really be happy spending the rest of my life with him? Up until a few weeks ago, we couldn't stand to be in the same room with each other, more less share the same household.

Now my mother, after one look at Eric, thought he was a winner. Could I trust my mother's intuition? I disliked her husband Otis so why should I trust anything she said? Then again, she had been married practically her entire adult life so wisdom and experience were certainly on her side.

Maybe I should have talked to Lydia about my dilemma and gotten her take on my dating scenario. As much as I would have loved to get one-on-one with Lydia, I didn't want her to think I was a fool. Come on now! I've got an ex-boyfriend with alcoholic tendencies, a business partner who thinks he's God's gift to the world, and an employee with who I'd rather play a game of cards than snuggle up with, and I'm supposed to choose out of the three?

Frustrated with my lack of answers, I pulled myself up from the sofa and dragged my body up the stairs and onto my bed. I shut my eyes at the depressing thought that maybe none of these men were right for me. Maybe I just needed to get comfortable with being alone.

God, I hope you're not up there laughing at me. I probably am being the biggest fool and the answer is right in front of me, but I'm too blind to see it. You know my heart. You know I desire companionship. I honestly don't know what to do or who to choose and I am so afraid that I'll make the wrong choice. Please help me not to miss what you have for me. I really need you.

Ring. Ring.

At first I thought I was dreaming, but a quick glance over at the cordless phone on my night stand confirmed that the phone was in fact ringing. My eyes shuffled from the phone to the alarm clock next to it. 1:00 a.m. Who in all of God's creation was calling my house after hours?

Woozily, I reached over and picked up the phone. For the sake of the caller, it had better been an emergency because I had a few choice words lined up for whoever was disturbing my sleep.

"Hello," I answered groggily, not trying to disguise my sleepy voice.

"Amber, hey baby." It was Chris, and I was going to kill him.

"Chris, what's up? Why are you calling me so late? Is everything okay?"

"I was over here thinking about you. You haven't returned my phone calls."

Seriously? Did he seriously think that because I didn't return any of his calls during regular hours, that calling me in the middle of the night was the logical next choice? Ooh, I was ready to clobber him! "Look, I've been busy–"

"Hello?" Right when I was about to let him have it, my mom's voice infiltrated the conversation.

"Mom? I got it," I said feeling like a teenager getting busted on the phone after curfew.

"Amber, who is calling so late?" my mom intruded.

"Amber, your mom's in town? Why didn't you tell me?" Chris inquired.

My mom gasped at the sound of the male caller's voice. "Who is this? Is this Eric?"

"Mm." Chris moaned possessively. "So Amber, who is Eric? Is that the name of the guy you were out with a couple weeks ago?"

I laughed at Chris' audacity and my mother's nosiness. "No, Mom it's not Eric. Would you please hang up the phone?"

"Sorry, Mrs. Ross. I didn't know you were visiting your daughter. My name is Chris. I'm Amber's boyfriend."

"What? No, Mom. Chris is my ex-boyfriend."

Chris grunted. "Amber, I thought we were working on us."

"Actually, Chris, my last name is Austin. Mrs. Anita Austin. I remarried after Amber's father, Mr. Ross passed."

"Well then I apologize, Mrs. Austin. Nice to meet you, though."

"Likewise," my mother continued. "I know Amber is a grown woman, but you shouldn't be calling her house all hours of the night. The only thing open this late is legs. Have respect for Amber and call her during the day."

"I apologize, ma'am. I wasn't trying to disrespect your daughter. I just hadn't heard from her in several days and I was concerned."

"I understand, young man."

I couldn't believe this. Was I really on the phone at one o'clock in the morning with my mother and Chris? This foolishness had to end! "Mom! Hang up the phone or I'm taking it out of your room!"

My mother chuckled. "Testy, testy. Alright, I'm going back to bed. You all should, too. Good night.

"Good night, Mrs. Austin," Chris said.

"Night, Mom," I added.

The line clicked, indicating my mother had hung up.

"You shouldn't talk to your mom like that," Chris stated as if he had any right to chastise me.

I was livid. Why was I even bothering to communicate with someone who was never going to be the kind of man that I needed? "And you shouldn't call my house at one in the morning. Matter-of-fact, don't call my house or cell phone anymore. This isn't working for me."

"Huh? Amber, why are you tripping?"

"Chris, the only reason I let you back into my life is because I still care about you, but so much has changed, and I'm not the woman you left behind five months ago. I now realize that you're not the one for me, and I'm not the one for you. Whatever really happened between you and Noel, you need to deal with it and not come back to me as a rebound."

"Amber, don't be like that."

"Chris, there are other people in my life who are serious about me, and you're not. This is just a game for you. Let's just move on. I'm tired and I have to work in the morning so I'm going to say goodbye. Goodbye, Chris."

I didn't even wait for him to respond with a goodbye. Instead, I simply hung up the phone, rolled over in my bed, and pulled the covers over my head.

Attempting to dodge my mother, I tiptoed out of the house the next morning. I knew she would fire a dozen questions at me about Chris that I was not prepared or willing to answer. She had only been in town for less than twenty-four hours and was already making me feel like an adolescent in my own home. And to think, I still had six months to go.

Being around Eric at the office was a slightly different experience after my recent discussion with my mother about him. I found myself gawking at him absent mindedly, pondering if she was right. Was Eric really the guy for me? Were fireworks really necessary? Was that the secret to a lasting marriage that married women had been holding back all along; that chemistry comes later, not first? Eric was one of the best men I had ever known. I never saw him scouting out women to sleep around with. He was a Christian who seemed to uphold the values of the faith. He was respectful, kind, and generous, but as much as I adored all these things about him, there was a nagging voice in my head that told me something was missing from our relationship, that he wasn't good enough, that I should leave him alone. If I ended up with Eric, would I just be settling? No way. I refused to settle for less than I deserved.

After a long day of paperwork and phone calls, I was looking forward to going to the house and enjoying a home cooked meal. One of the perks of having my mother in town was that she was infamous for her soul food and believed in preparing a hot meal on a daily basis. Driving home I could almost taste her hot water cornbread in my mouth. Yum!

When I pulled into my driveway, I was taken aback by a sparkling silver Jaguar already consuming space in my driveway. The woman had only been here a day and already had visitors, really? I fumbled with unlocking the front door, my impatience brewing. All I wanted to do was come home to some good food and chill. Now, I would have to wear a fake smile while some folks that I didn't know and didn't want in my house ate up my food and infringed upon my abode. Momma and I were going to have to have a talk about house rules before this got out of control.

I briskly entered the foyer, tossed my purse down on the console, skipped checking voicemails because I was positive my mother had answered all of my calls, and headed straight for the dining room, the scent of black eyed peas and rice greeting me along the way. I could hear voices and laughter coming from the dining room, infuriating me even more. How are you going to be "Ha-Ha-Ha-ing" all up in my house?

I sharply turned the corner and came to a screeching halt.

Sitting in my dining room, scooping up a forkful of my momma's greens was none other than Jonathan Gold. Why did this man love to spring up in places he shouldn't be? I gritted my teeth. Gold had some stalker tendencies that we were going to have to talk about A.S.A.P.

"Hey honey," my mom said when she noticed I had entered the room. "We were wondering when you would get home. I was just telling your friend Jonathan about the time you peed on yourself in high school."

This is the reason why people never want their parents to meet their friends. Why would she tell Gold about one of the most embarrassing moments of my life? Okay, to clear up the matter, it's not as bad as it sounds. I was in the 9th grade, we had to take some crazy standardized test that took like three hours, and the stupid proctor wouldn't let us go to the bathroom. I had awakened late that morning and rushed out the door without my usual morning urinary release. By the time I was an hour into the exam, my bladder was aching so bad I thought I was going to burst. I pleaded with the man giving the test to let me go, but thinking I was trying to cheat, he refused. When I finally was allowed to go, two hours later, I made it only halfway down the hall before the floodgates broke. As you see, peeing on myself wasn't my fault.

My eyes narrowed. "Mom! Are you trying to humiliate me?"

She waved me away. "Of course not! Stop being so dramatic."

I rolled my eyes because it was evident that she wasn't playing fair. "Anyways," I shifted my focus to Gold who was stuffing potato salad into his mouth like this was Thanksgiving, "Wh-what are you doing here?"

He picked up his napkin from the table and wiped his mouth before speaking. "Amber, don't get upset with your mother. We were just swapping memories about you."

"Yeah, that certainly makes me feel a lot better," I responded sarcastically. "What are you doing here?"

"Oh, sorry. I called you at the office, and you weren't there so I figured I would swing by and invite you out to dinner, but when I got here, your mom had already cooked this delicious feast and invited me to stay. Sit down and join us." He tapped the empty chair next to him as if I were a dog who would obediently oblige him.

I put my left hand on my hip in true sista-girl fashion. "Gold, I do not need you to invite me to dinner at my own house, eating off my plates, with food prepared in my kitchen, using groceries that I bought with my own money."

"Amber, you're being rude and childish," my mother intervened.

I looked at my mom like she had just grown horns and had a pitchfork in her hand. Me? Childish? Oh, she hadn't seen anything yet. "Okay, that's it! Mom, I love you, I truly do, but we are going to have to establish some boundaries if this is going to work. Number one, please don't answer my phone. You have a cell phone so no one is calling you at my house. Whenever that phone rings, it is for me, so let me handle it. Number two, you may not like the way I deal with people, but I'm a grown woman. This is me. Yes, I'm not always the nicest person in the world, but people don't respond to nice people. The reason I am successful is because I know how to make others respect me."

"Now Amber, you shouldn't speak to your mother like that." Otis interjected; too busy feeding his face to really defend my mother.

I sucked my teeth and gave him a don't-start-none-won't-be-none look. "Otis, these rules apply to you too."

Gold reached out for my free hand, but I yanked it back. "Amber I didn't mean to cause friction between you and your parents."

I looked around the table, all three sets of eyes glaring at me like I was the antichrist. I sighed heavily because no matter what I said or did, I wasn't going to win this battle. Once again, my mother had outwitted me. "No, I didn't mean to interrupt your wonderful meal. Continue. I'm going out for Chinese."

I jumped in my truck and sped away from the house like I was auditioning for the movie *The Fast and the Furious*. Immediately, I began to feel remorseful about my adult temper tantrum. I didn't know what it was, but my mother and Otis seemed to bring the worst out of me. I should have probably gone back home and apologized, but my pride wouldn't let me. Gold had to think I was straight loony, but a part of me didn't care. Like my mother told me the night prior, the man for me would want me regardless of the ugly sides of me. Gold would just have to take it or leave it.

I knew I needed to learn to be more patient with my mother and Otis. The Wife 101 class had taught me to be a woman of goodness and kindness. I had been working on being a gentler person, but with the arrival of Mr. and Mrs. Austin a.k.a. "the folks," all my hard work fell apart. A lot of prayer. That's exactly what I needed to get through this emotional roadblock.

I picked up my phone, looking for a sympathetic ear. Tisha loved her some Momma Anita; calling her would make me feel like a complete monster. So, I called the only other "Team Amber" member I knew, Eric.

He picked up on the fourth ring, laughing as if he were at the Uptown Comedy Corner. "Hey, Boss!"

"Eric, thank God you answered. I'm having a mommy meltdown."

"Already? You and your momma don't waste any time, huh?"

"If you only knew."

"Where are you now?"

"Driving down 75/85 as if I don't have a home. I just had to get out of there, and I'm so mad because I'm missing out on her finger licking good soul food."

"Well come over here. We've got plenty."

"We? Where are you?"

"I'm at my parent's place out in Conyers."

"I don't want to impose."

"No imposition at all. It's my father's birthday so a few family members and friends stopped by the house. One more is no problem. I'll text you the directions. When you get here, you can tell me all about it over macaroni and cheese, fried chicken, and peach cobbler."

I smiled. Eric always seemed to know how to brighten my day. "Okay. You got me with the peach cobbler. I'm on my way."

I arrived a little over thirty minutes later. Eric had lied. There were way more than a few family members and friends at his parents' house. Over fifty people were spread out between the kitchen, living room, dining room, and the finished and furnished basement. I got to meet all of the key people in his life including his parents, siblings, uncles, aunts, cousins, and even his daughter Jonelle. Jonelle was sweet, but I could tell that she also was a spoiled little princess by her sassy pink outfit with a matching purse. When she met me, she looked at me a little skeptically, as if to warn me not to hurt her daddy. I winked at her to let her know I understood and would be on my best behavior. She then relaxed and pulled a tube of glittery, pink lip gloss from her purse and proceeded to freshen up her lips. I guess she wanted to let me know that she was the prettiest chick at the party. I didn't challenger her; I just let her have the crown.

Eric's sisters and mom welcomed me with open arms while his brother and father scrutinized me and gave him a hard time.

"So you're the one who has my son working all kinds of crazy hours?" his father, Dwayne, grilled me in front of Eric and the rest of his family.

I finished swallowing a chunk of peach cobbler. "Guilty as charged, but if he would have told me that you all cooked like this, I would have scheduled more work meetings at home–here at your home!"

We all laughed.

"Thanks, sweetheart. There is plenty of food so eat as much as you like," his mother, Ernestine, chimed in.

"Don't let him fool you, Amber. He is just trying to butter you up for a raise!" his brother, Nelson, joked.

I giggled and smiled at Eric who was shrugging his shoulders like he'd been caught. "I know. I'm onto his game. What he doesn't know is that I'm getting ready to hire one of those illegal immigrants to take over his job. Those Mexicans are no joke. They can do in two days what it takes him a week to do, and only for fifty cents a day!"

Eric pouted. "See, that's wrong! Don't make me call the feds on you. I can be a whistleblower. Try me!"

"Please don't fire him!" his sister, Karyn, pleaded. "Girl, he would be trying to come live with me, and he doesn't know how to pick up his nasty draws from the floor!"

"Amen to that! I already got three kids to raise, which includes my husband. I can't handle anymore, family or not!" his sister, Cindy, hooted.

"Yeah, Eric. You're not welcomed back here either. You might have to go stay at one of those shelters downtown," Mr. Hayes announced playfully.

Eric waved his arms to stop all the fun we were having at his expense. "All right, alright now! Break it up. I can tell this is the last time I'm going to bring anyone home because y'all don't know how to act! Treatin' a brotha all bad. You too, Amber."

Eric's family knew how to have fun. I joined in the festivities of playing bid whiz, dancing to 70's music, and laughing at old family photos. I couldn't help but inwardly envy the relationship Eric had with his people. I'd always fantasized about being a part of a clan like this, but my reality was so far from this picture perfect example.

Two and a half hours later, Eric and I sat alone in the living room watching some low budget horror flick. Most of the crowd had dispersed, but a few stragglers were making to-go plates and saying their final farewells.

Eric nudged me on the shoulder, stealing my attention away from the screaming victim on the movie. "So what happened with your mom today?"

I sheepishly looked down at my hands. "Nothing. It's stupid."

"That's okay. Tell me anyway." He turned his body towards me to signify that I had his full attention.

"Well, it sort of began last night. I got a phone call in the middle of the night and my mother got on the phone and is telling the caller that it was too late to be calling my house as if I'm fifteen or something."

He chuckled. "She had a point, but that had to be embarrassing."

"Yeah, it was. Then today I come home to find her sitting around the dining room table with Jonathan Gold, telling him about humiliating experiences from my childhood. When I flipped out, everyone looked at me as if I was the bad guy."

He raised his eyebrows. "Wow. Not to be nosy but why was Mr. Gold at your house?"

Again, I would have to lie to Eric which I hated. Well maybe not a full lie, just a half lie. A white lie? Don't say it, I know. A lie is a lie, but Eric wasn't ready for the truth.

"Who knows? I wasn't expecting him or anything; he just kind of showed up, but Gold is like that. He probably just wanted to go over some numbers. This Green Global thing is a mess."

"I thought it was going well. What's changed?"

I shrugged my shoulder. "Nothing and everything. They still aren't giving us the conditions we need on our contract. I think they are used to dealing with people less experienced than us so they are trying to pull the wool over our eyes. Plus, I have this sinking suspicion that they're a little slimy. I'm just waiting on having my instincts confirmed before I make a big deal about it."

Eric grinned and caressed my forearm softly. "You're a smart woman. I am sure if there is anything shady going on, you'll figure it out before it's too late. Don't be afraid to trust God on this one. And when it comes to your mom, just remember that she loves you and this is the only way she knows how to show it. I know you still have some leftover frustrations from your childhood, but you have to forgive and let it go. You are an adult now. You don't have to stay in that bad emotional place anymore. Do you get what I'm saying?"

I nodded. "Yeah. Yeah, I do. You're right. It's so hard though. It's like my emotions get the best of me and next thing I know I am saying something that I end up regretting. I don't want to be disrespectful; I just want her to accept me for who I am."

"Well, you can't ask for what you're unwilling to give. If you want her to accept you, you are going to have to first learn to accept her."

When I walked into my house around 11 p.m. that night, my mom was waiting up for me in the kitchen. Eric had given me some food for thought, and I was still munching on it. I wanted my relationship with my mother to be better, but I just couldn't seem to tame my indignant emotions. She knew how to push my buttons, how to make me be someone I loathed. If I was going to move on to a higher place in my life, I would have to forgive her. I only wished I knew how.

"Hey, Mom," I mumbled as I walked into the kitchen and saw her sitting at the table, drinking a cup of tea and reading a copy of *National Geographic* magazine.

She put down the magazine and gazed up at me. "Hi, honey. Are you hungry? I put the food in the fridge, but I can always take it out and make you a plate."

I forced a smile. "No, I ate. But thanks…When did Gold leave?"

"Gold?"

"Jonathan. That's his last name, Gold. His name is Jonathan Gold. I don't know why but we call each other by our last names. He kind of started calling me Ross first, and I just returned the sentiment by calling him Gold and then….It's silly. It's not important."

"Oh, okay. Well, he left shortly after you did." She took a sip of tea, blowing on the liquid in the course.

I sat down across from her at the table, determined to clear the air. "Uh, Ma, I'm sorry that I haven't been the nicest host so far. I just have a lot of things that I need to work out within myself."

She chuckled to herself. "I accept your apology. For some reason, you and I have never been able to see eye-to-eye. To be honest, sometimes I think that you don't like me very much."

I gasped. "I love you, Mom! You know I love you."

She shook her head. "I know you love me, but do you like me? Love and like are two entirely different things."

"I guess you're right. Hmm, I never thought about it like that. I want to like you, but I really don't understand you."

"What's not to understand?"

"Why you insist on treating me like a child? Or why you always have to be so dependent on a man?"

"I don't mean to treat you like a child, but no matter how old you are, you will always be my baby. I remember the first time I held you in my arms. You were so beautiful and determined. You still are." She paused and smiled at the thought then continued, "As for me and men, I like being loved and supported by a man. Yeah, I could survive without one, but why? I know you have never cared for Otis, but he is a good man. He was there for me when I was coping with the death of your father. I was a mess, and he loved me. I'm still a mess, and he still loves me. He may be difficult at times, but I know his heart is in the right place. Baby, I understand that you've been fighting not to end up like me, but in the process, you are keeping yourself from being you and being happy."

I swallowed, feeling ridiculous for my complaints. "I guess I won't be winning any awards for Daughter of the Year."

She placed her hand over top of mine. "Don't think like that. I meant it when I told you how proud I am of you. And it's not about the money, house, or businesses. It's because you've grown into an intelligent woman who is not afraid to try. Most people never live life to the fullest because they're too afraid to simply try."

I wrapped my finger around hers and gave her hand a light squeeze. "Thanks, Mom."

She squeezed my hand back then pulled away. "Now that we've gotten that out of the way, you know how your momma is. Who is Chris and why is he calling your house in the middle of the night like he don't got no sense? And what's going on with you and Jonathan because he is definitely up to something?"

I laughed. "I knew it was coming. Some things never change! Okay the truth is…I've been dating three guys at once."

"Now you know I didn't raise you like that. Amber!" She covered her mouth in shock.

I ran my right hand through my hair. "It's not like it sounds. Eric was the first one who approached me and told me he was interested. I like him, but he is my employee so I wasn't sure about the whole office dating thing. While I was thinking about it, Gold, I mean Jonathan, who is a potential business partner and who hated me, all of a sudden tells me he likes me too. While I was trying to sort out those two, Chris, who is my ex-boyfriend who was supposed to be getting married to someone else comes back into my life begging for another chance…It still sounds bad, doesn't it?" I cringed and held my breath as I awaited her response.

She sucked her teeth. "Mm Hmm. So whatcha gonna do? You can't keep stringing these guys along."

"Why not? Men do it all the time." See, I can't help being a little rebellious!

"Amber!"

"Yeah, yeah. I'm kidding! Well, it's not an easy decision. Chris and I have history. I actually wanted to marry him before he dumped me. But now, I'm not feeling him. I care about him, but have a feeling he's just using me as a rebound. The fact that he wanted to marry someone else and now wants me back seems off. He won't tell me exactly what happened with the woman he was supposed to marry which really makes me suspicious. I told him last night after you hung up to stop calling me so I guess my choice is really down to two."

She sipped her tea again. "Okay. Go on."

"Gold is like my ideal man, so to speak. He is rich, successful, good looking, and he is already telling people he's going to marry me. It's like he is the male version of me. Very ambitious, very strong."

"But?"

"But I feel like it's almost too perfect. Like everything is plastic and fake, sort of a façade. I don't want to be married for ten years and wake up one day not knowing who I am or who I married."

"He told me and Otis that he planned to marry you." Another sip.

I leaned forward. "He did what? I don't know why I'm acting surprised. That is a classic Gold move."

"And what about Eric?" Sip. Sip.

I exhaled and sat back. "Eric is wonderful. I love being around Eric. I am so comfortable with him, but sometimes I feel that we are better off as friends. I'm not sure if I can handle more with him. We are in two different places in life, he has a kid, and I just don't know how it would work. So that's it in a nutshell. I know you're going to give me your opinion so go on and say it."

She took one last sip and placed the mug down on the table. "You have two men who are serious about you. It's as easy as deciding what you need in a man and which one can really give you what you need. If you need your match, Gold is it. But if you need a companion that's also a friend, Eric is the one. I can't tell you who to choose, but don't wait too long or you might not have anyone left to pick from."

Lesson 20: Be Prepared

She makes fine linen garments and leads others to buy them; she delivers to the merchants girdles [or sashes that free one up for service]. Strength and dignity are her clothing and her position is strong and secure; she rejoices over the future [the latter day or time to come, knowing that she and her family are in readiness for it]!

(Proverbs 31: 24-25)

The rest of the week went off without a hitch. I made more of an effort to get along with my mother and Otis, and they tried to respect my house rules. On Saturday, I took them to visit the Coca Cola Museum and the Georgia Aquarium, and on Sunday, they went with me to church. I even told my mother about the Wife 101 course I'd been taking and what I had learned so far. She was impressed and encouraged me to see it all the way through. Because I had cut Chris off, and Gold and Eric knew my parents were in town, I didn't have to worry about going out on any dates, which was fine by me. I needed time to figure out which guy I was going to get serious with before one found out about the other. By the time Monday's class rolled around, I was desperately in need of some godly wisdom to help me make such a major decision.

"Proverbs 31:24 reads, 'She makes fine linen garments and leads others to buy them; she delivers to the merchants girdles or sashes that free one up for service.' This verse speaks of the entrepreneurial spirit of the virtuous woman." Lydia began the class finally talking about something I could completely relate to: business.

"One thing that I believe hurts a lot of us in today's society is that we rely too much on traditional employment to make ends meet. Not that there is anything wrong with holding a nine-to-five, but we limit ourselves to these jobs and in the process disable ourselves. When economic hard times come, we find that we have not developed other skills and talents outside of our jobs, thereby making it harder to survive. In my opinion, we should all have a few side hustles, ways to make money outside of employment."

This topic was right up my alley, so for the first time in a long time, I didn't feel overwhelmed by the virtuous woman. I nodded my head in agreement, glad that the virtuous woman and Lydia were finally on my side.

Lydia looked down at her bible. "Verse twenty-four expresses this woman's ability to make and sell things. It demonstrates her ability to be innovative as well as persuasive. What is interesting is that there is the potential for her to make money in three different ways. First, she makes linen garments and can sell them directly to people herself. She could have her own store at the market, or she can sell out of her house. Second and third, she delivers sashes to the merchants. She might sell the sashes directly to the merchants for their own use, or on the other hand, she might act as the merchants' sash distributor and sell to the merchants at wholesale prices so that the merchants can sell them at retail to the public. Any way you look at the matter, this woman has a business and a way to make money if needed."

I was elated. The virtuous woman was more like me than I imagined. I had three businesses; she had three businesses, sort of.

"Another important aspect of this verse that I would like to point out is that this is the only verse in this chapter that talks about her doing any of her tasks for monetary gain. As we have studied, we've seen this woman work hard at home and in her community, but it has never indicated that any of the things she was doing was for pay. However, verse twenty-four says that she leads others to buy what she makes; buy signifying that she is getting some sort of compensation for her items. I believe the significance of only one mention of compensation is similar to our discussion of verse twenty-two. Although she has this business and opportunity to make money, she doesn't spend all of her time focusing on them. Her life is so much more than making money. Her life is balanced; selling things and monetary gain are only two small aspects of what makes her a wonderful woman, wife, and mother. She does not define herself by her business or money, and neither do others."

I should have known there was a "but" coming! Just when Miss Perfect and I were starting to understand each other, she shows up with something called "balance."

Lydia rubbed her chin with her left hand. "This is a lesson we could all learn a lot from. How not to define ourselves by our jobs, positions, or the money we make or don't make. Our society is very superficial and materialistic. We like to look at people's bank accounts and decide whether or not they are special by what is or isn't in them. When someone makes or has a lot of money, we view them as important, but when someone has less financially, we pity them and treat them with less respect. Money is just money. It comes and it goes. There are rich people who used to be poor and poor people who used to be rich. Money is not a stable enough concept to build opinions, attitudes, or reputations upon. How can I define myself or anyone else by an item that may or may not be there tomorrow? We have to start basing our definitions of ourselves on the only permanent thing in this world, and that is God. The Lord is the only One who is constant, consistent, and credible. Everything and everyone else will eventually pass away."

Whoa! So did that mean I should choose Eric over Gold? Was I defining Eric and Gold by their net worth? More importantly, was I defining myself by the dollars in my bank account? Was it that I thought people like myself and Gold were better than the Erics of this world? *But I thought we were supposed to be compatible, equally yoked, and all that other good stuff? Oh Lord, what does all of this mean?*

Before I could come up with an answer, Lydia continued her lesson, forcing me to lose my train of thought. "Verse twenty-five reads, 'Strength and dignity are her clothing and her position is strong; she rejoices over the future, the latter day or time to come, knowing that she and her family are in readiness for it!' Now I know that in our society we get consumed with name brand clothing. We feel good about ourselves when we are wearing clothing from stores like Anne Taylor, The Limited, Nordstrom's, Bloomingdale's, or Macy's. There is nothing wrong with shopping at these stores or wearing nice clothes, but contrary to popular belief, clothes don't make the woman. What is on the inside will always be revealed on the outside. I don't care how much you dress yourself up, if who you are ugly or weak on the inside, you inner character will override anything you are physically wearing."

So, she is just gonna list all of my favorite stores, huh? Okay, I knew this message was for me. First the business and money part and now shopping and clothes? God, You are a trip!

"The virtuous woman has good stuff within her. She doesn't have to wear the flashiest clothing to get people to notice her. She can come outside in a pair of sweatpants and a t-shirt, and people will still see her as the sharpest woman around. Have you ever noticed that when you are all dressed up that no one says anything to you, but when you walk out of the house in a pair of jeans and a wrinkled shirt, that is when someone compliments you? That is because it is not about what's on the outside that truly shines through. Often when you are dressed from head-to-toe, people cannot see you because they are so distracted by the glitz-n-glam. But when you get down to basic clothing, a-ha! There is where the beauty resides.

"Strength and dignity are her clothing. When you see her, no matter what she is wearing physically, you see a strong and dignified person. You see someone you respect, someone you can trust, someone you look up to. Her position is strong. You don't have to worry about her being fickle. Tomorrow when you see her, she'll be wearing strength and dignity again. She is always on her A-game. When you see her in two weeks or a year from now, she'll be adorned in strength and dignity."

Lydia let out a short giggle as if she and God had an inside joke going on. "Someone who possesses all of these wonderful characteristics enjoys life and looks forward to what's next. If I know that I am being the best person that I can be and living the best life that I can live, I don't have to be afraid of what tomorrow holds. Tomorrow should be another good day because I am living in my maximum potential. Even if something bad happens tomorrow, I don't have to fret because I know that everything will work out in the end because I am doing everything I am supposed to be doing. A lot of times when we get nervous and wonder if something bad will happen to us, it is because we know deep down inside that we aren't doing everything we're supposed to be doing. For example, if I'm in school and I'm reading my textbook and studying my lessons and paying attention in class and doing my homework, I don't have to worry about whether or not I'll pass the next test or complete the class. I've done my part. I'm prepared. Pop quiz? I'm ready. Final exam? Bring it on! However, if I'm not reading, studying, or paying attention, yes, I'm nervous about that next quiz or test. A woman of virtue can be excited and joyful about the future because she is prepared, and she has prepared her family for it. She has done her part."

As I was gathering my things at the end of class, Lydia walked over to me to greet me personally. A few weeks had passed since she last singled me out, so I thought I had escaped her attention, but at that moment, looking at her gaze, I knew she was still on to me.

"Good evening, Miss Ross. What did you think about the class tonight?"

I slid my notebook into my tote bag and swung it over my shoulder. "Good evening, Mrs. Woods. I enjoyed the class, but I always do."

"Wonderful. Are you learning anything?" She smiled expectantly.

"Oh yes. I've learned so much. Who knew Proverbs 31 was so insightful and relative to life in the modern world?"

"That's the thing with God's Word. We may change, but it never does. The bible is full of lessons that still apply to us today as they did thousands of years ago."

I nodded. "Very true. I appreciate you taking the time to teach us how to be better women. I think I'm slowly getting there."

She tilted her head slightly, showing interest. "Oh. Good. Do you mean that from a personal standpoint, or is there someone special in your life? I know you told me you weren't married, but are you dating?"

I wiggled a bit, feeling put on the spot. "I'm kind of dating. I guess you could say I'm weighing my options."

I suppose she noticed my discomfort because she seemed to ease up. "I see. Well, I will keep you in my prayers that God will direct your steps. And as I told you before, you are welcome to call me anytime. Do you still have my number?"

I nodded again quickly. "Yes. I have it."

"Don't be afraid to use it." She placed her right hand on my shoulder blade and stepped closer as if she was preparing to tell me a secret. "One of the biggest lessons I've learned in relationships is the importance of having the counsel of godly women. There are a lot of people who will listen to your problems and even give you advice that seems logical, but that doesn't mean it's the truth or the right thing to do. As humans, the things that we think and believe are so far off from the way God thinks and knows. His thoughts and ways are not like ours. That's why we have to trust Him and not lean to our own understanding.

"What makes sense to us is not always His way of doing things. For example, the world tells us if your husband or wife isn't making you happy, divorce them, but that's not God's way. It's not about whether we are happy every day; it's about honoring the commitment we made to God and our spouses. This is why as women we need wise, god-fearing women in our life who can remind us of God's plan and not our own. Does that make sense?"

"A lot! And you're right. I've had some decisions I needed to make and talking to other people wound up giving me a headache. Everyone has an opinion, but I still find myself unsure of what I should do."

"Like I said, call me if you want to talk about it. I am willing to pray with you and help you seek God's will in the matter."

"Thanks. I will keep that in mind." I was tempted to spill my guts to her right then and there, but for some reason I clammed up. Instead, I wished her a good night and left. At least I knew that if push came to shove, I could call her with all of my drama. Lydia Woods was now officially on Team Amber.

Lesson 21: The Truth Shall Set You Free

And you will know the Truth, and the Truth will set you free. (John 8:32)

Just when my life was starting to make sense, all hell broke loose. I don't like a lot of drama, I really don't, but it seemed that drama followed me like gnats follow sweaty people in the summer. Wouldn't it be nice just to go to work, come home, and chill without all the extra stuff? Constant peace would be nice, but then again, life without a bit of drama, wouldn't be human life at all.

The drama started on Thursday when my people-who-know-people called me back with the intel I'd been waiting to hear about Green Global. It was late in the day, and I was finishing up at the office when my cell phone buzzed.

"This is Amber Ross," I answered coolly as I snapped the flip phone open.

"I got that information you've been wanting. I'm emailing it to you now. You're not going to be happy. Let me know if you need anything else," the caller rambled before hanging up without a goodbye.

I took a deep breath and logged on to my email, slightly afraid, but mostly curious, about what I would find out about the natural food store chain. The email appeared at the top of my inbox with the subject line, Green Global. I opened the email and read:

SOME THINGS YOU MIGHT WANT TO KNOW. SEE ATTACHMENT.

Immediately, I downloaded the attached file and read it with urgency. Being shaken by its contents, I read it again, but this time slower to make sure I hadn't missed anything. I hadn't. There in plain black, typed font, were good reasons why we should walk away from the Green Global deal and never look back. I printed out a few copies of the file so that I could provide Perkins and Gold with the same information that I had. While the printer did its thing, I did mine.

"Hey babe!" Gold enthusiastically addressed me as he answered his phone. We'd had a few phone conversations since the big blow up at my house, and he had acted as if everything was okay between us. We never officially spoke about the incident, but if he didn't think it was crucial to bring it up, I wouldn't either.

I pulled the printed documents out of the printer's tray and visually glossed them over. "We need to meet. Perkins, too. I got some not-so-good-news to share about our boys over at Green Global."

"Really? I see. Well, come by the office in an about an hour. I'll let Perkins know."

"Okay." I could hear in his voice a bit of resistance, but like it or not, I had to tell them the truth. My biggest concern was Perkins. He was the one who first came up with the Green Global idea and, therefore, had invested the most energy into making sure the deal happened. If we pulled out now, he would take the biggest hit monetarily and professionally. I expected him to fight me on this one; I just wasn't sure how nasty his objections would be.

An hour and a half later, I found out. We sat in the small conference room at Perkins & Gold Investments in midtown Atlanta. Their office, nestled on the 9th floor of a newly constructed downtown high-rise building on Peachtree, offered the feel of a company destined to be a Fortune 500. As the men reviewed the document I provided them, I gazed out of the window at the steady flow of six o'clock traffic and the hustle of corporate types scrambling to make it to happy hour.

The sound of paper hitting the conference room table caused me to turn around and face them. Disappointment covered their faces like a tightly knit ski cap. Perkins tapped his pen loudly against the mahogany table out of frustration and the fact that there was nothing else more aggressive he could do that wouldn't cost him more money.

Ending the silence, I leaned in and let out a huff. "Green Global is not the morally committed company they claim to be. The fact that its top executives are affiliated with sweatshops in third world nations and biochemical waste corporations says how they really feel about the world. They have several legal issues that have been swept under the rug, including embezzlement and extortion. It honestly appears that the only reason that Green Global exists is as a smokescreen for all their other infractions. I know we've put a lot into this deal, but we simply cannot do business with them."

Perkins' face hardened. "Where did you get this information from?"

"I can't say, but I know it's legit. Let's just say I know people who know people." I had always wanted to say that line to someone. I loved that secretive, mafia type stuff.

"You know people who know people? What kind of horse manure is that?" Perkins scowled.

Oops! Maybe that wasn't the right time to insert a movie line. Yeah, this was going to be real ugly. I put my game face on and looked Perkins square in the eyes. "The kind that will keep us out of trouble. It doesn't matter who my source is. What does matter is that the truth of who we are dealing with is right here on this piece of paper. Now we can heed to the warning and get out now. Or we can take a huge risk and end up mixed up in a bunch of 'horse manure' in the future."

Gold jumped in as the mediator, which was weird because that job was usually held by Perkins. "Ross, I understand your concerns and looking at this document, you have every right to feel worried, but I also see Perkins' side on this. We've put too much into this deal just to walk away right now. As much as this news is bad, it really has nothing to do with us starting a grocery store in Atlanta."

I gasped at Gold as if I had just witnessed him grow vampire fangs. "Nothing to do with us? Are you serious?"

"Yes. What the Green Global execs do on their time is their business, not ours."

I gazed at Gold and then at Perkins and saw that despite my hardcore proof, they weren't trying to hear me. I would have to try a different approach. "Gold and Perkins, both of you are extremely intelligent and talented businessmen, which has a lot to do with your success thus far. I'll give you that. But don't be foolish. What Green Global does has everything to do with us if we get into bed with them. If they go down for reckless business practices, everyone connected to them will be labeled and put on the chopping block. Not only that, when you lie down with dogs, you get up with fleas. If these people would conduct unsavory business practices with others, they will also do the same to us. We need to bail now."

Perkins' face turned beet red. That was his problem; he didn't have a poker face. I could read him loud and clear, and there was absolutely nothing I could say to change his mind. He confirmed my assumption when he replied, "Ross, as much as we appreciate your Spike Lee Do-the-Right-Thing speech, we are not pulling out of this deal. I have put up with a lot of your antics over the course of this deal, but this stops right here. Now, if you don't want to move forward, let us know, and we will unfortunately have to find a replacement for you."

Gold grabbed my hand sympathetically, not wanting me to take Perkins' comment personally. "Ross, please just take some time to think about it. We don't want to lose you."

I picked up my shoulder bag, slid my copy of the document into it, zipped it closed, and stood up. I wasn't angry, but I also didn't like being given an ultimatum. However, being the cool-headed professional that I am with the best poker face in town, I nodded gracefully and said, "Maybe we should all take some time to think about this." Without waiting for a response, I walked out of the door.

By the time I entered my house that evening, I had a massive headache. My entire drive home, I had spent ruminating about the Green Global disaster. I didn't want to desert Perkins and Gold, but at the same time I didn't feel comfortable proceeding with the contract. One of the most important qualities to have in the business world was a good reputation, and I had built all of my companies on my good name. I wasn't willing to allow scum like the Green Global execs to tarnish what had taken me a decade and over a million dollars to create.

I was grateful that my mom and Otis had gone out for dinner and a movie because I needed some alone time. I cracked open a bottle of ibuprofen, took three, and plopped down off the sofa, my favorite chill spot. As I began to feel the drug kicking in and my body starting to relax, the piercing sound of the doorbell ringing brought the thumping in my skull back to full force.

Begrudgingly, I crawled off the couch, headed to the door, and yanked it open.

"Have you lost your everlasting mind? You don't show up to my house all willie-nillie without calling! What do you want?" I'll admit; I can be a bit mean, and I had been praying that God would help me bear the Fruit of the Spirit having to do with kindness and gentleness. However, when that man showed up at my door unannounced and I already had a splitting headache, all of my religion and good intentions went out the door.

Chris was standing on the other side of the door looking like he had been hit by an Amtrak train, twice. He reeked of alcohol and appeared as if he had forgotten what a shower felt like. "Amber, baby. Baby please. Please just let me in."

I cut my eyes at him. "Oh he–...See, you almost made me curse! You can't come in my house. You need to go on with that 'baby please' mess. You smell like you've been doing the breaststroke in a pool filled with Vodka!"

He reached for my waist. "But I love you. Don't you love me?"

I pulled away from him like he had leprosy. "You don't love me. What you love is having me there to pick up the pieces Noel left behind."

"That's not true."

"Yes, it is. Be a man and tell me the truth. Why did you and Noel cancel the wedding?"

"I told you–"

I cut him off. "Tell me the truth!"

He looked at me with pain in his eyes. "You want to know the truth. The truth is that she…she…"

"She's what?" I edged him on.

"She's gay," he said dejectedly.

I didn't think I heard him correctly. "She's gay?"

He repeated himself. "She's gay. She's a lesbian. Well, not really. She's bisexual. She told me that she only agreed to marry me so that her family would get off her back. But she wants an open marriage. She already has a girlfriend and wants me to be okay with her continuing to see this woman after we get married. How can I compete with another woman? A man, I can understand, but a woman? I'm not letting my wife run around town with a woman. What kind of man would that make me?" He rubbed his face abrasively with his hands as if that would alter the situation.

I gulped, not knowing how to console him. "I'm sorry to hear that, I really am, but drinking yourself into a stupor is not going to solve your problems."

He looked up at me pleadingly. "I just need you to hold me."

As much as I felt bad for him, I also felt so angry. It was like I thought; he didn't want me, he just wanted a backup for Noel. "I can't do that. What happened to me being too independent and not letting a man be a man? What happened to all of that?"

"You tell me. You've changed. You're still bossy, but you've softened up some. You let me take you out and pay the bill. You let me lead the conversations and call you. You act as if everything that happens between us is up to me, like I'm the one who needs to get in where I fit in. You're not so desperate anymore, but you're also not acting like the whole I-don't-need-no-man thing either. I look at you now, and I don't know what has happened in the matter of a couple months, but I wish you would have been this way before. Maybe it would have been you and me getting married instead of me and Noel."

My mind flashed back to that day at lunch with him and his engagement party. I was grateful that his rejection of me led to me taking the Wife 101 class and working on becoming a better me. But I'm a firm believer of leaving the past in the past and the past included Chris.

"Thanks for noticing the changes in me, but I can't do this thing with you anymore. You can't just walk in and out of my life when you feel like it. I'm sorry I wasn't good enough for you back then, but now you're not good enough for me. I hope you find a way to get over Noel and that it is not found in a bottle. Please leave."

"Amber," he begged.

I put my hand up to silence him. "I'm going into my house now. If you ring my doorbell again, I'm calling the cops. You and I both know that I live in a predominately white neighborhood, and I'll put on my 'white voice' and have Atlanta's finest here in five seconds flat. So I advise you to leave now and avoid spending the night in Fulton County Jail." Nonchalantly, I closed the door and reclaimed my spot on the sofa.

Lesson 22: If You Don't Have Something Nice To Say...

She opens her mouth in skillful and godly Wisdom, and on her tongue is the law of kindness [giving counsel and instruction]. She looks well to how things go in her household, and the bread of idleness (gossip, discontent, and self-pity) she will not eat. (Proverbs 31:26-27)

"When I was young, people used to say, 'If you don't have something nice to say, don't say anything at all.' I would like to take that saying a step further and make it, 'If you don't have something nice *and* wise to say, don't say anything at all.' Here's why: Proverbs 31:26 reads, 'She opens her mouth in skillful and godly wisdom, and on her tongue is the law of kindness, giving counsel and instruction.' It is this verse right here where a lot of us women fall short."

Four days later, I was back in the Wife 101 class, listening to the sound of Lydia's voice. I guess Chris had gotten the message loud and clear because he did not ring my doorbell again that night and had not attempted to reach me since. I was still stressed about the Green Global situation, but that was because I still didn't have the courage to desert Gold and Perkins. I was known to be quite loyal, so often letting go had been a bit of a process. The decision of whom to date between Eric and Gold was also still up in the air, but I was slowly growing fonder of Eric. Getting to know his family and being able to share my mother issues with him sealed our bond, making him the likelier candidate, but the jury was still out. One wrong move, and either man could be booted to the curb alongside Chris.

Lydia, dressed in a long black skirt, white button down shirt, and black Mary Jane shoes, spoon fed us another big heaping lesson on godly womanhood. "As women, we like to talk a lot, especially more than men. There is a statistic floating around that women use at least seven to eight thousand more words a day than men do. Of course, this statistic does not reflect all men or all women, but it does point out a tendency in women to talk more than men. When you are a person who talks a lot, it is easy just to start rambling about any thought or idea that comes to mind. Your ability to censor your words or evaluate what you say becomes limited. So if an unkind thought comes in your mind or a foolish idea crosses your mind, it is more likely to be spoken. I'm not saying men don't speak unkindly or foolishly because we all know that is not true. What I am saying is that unkind and foolish words often start with the inability to tame your tongue. The more you allow yourself to speak without censorship, the more likely to speak harshly and unwisely."

This lesson certainly was one I needed to learn. I thought back to the way I dealt with Chris and felt slightly guilty. After the way he treated me in the past, he deserved to be ushered to the door, but I could have taken the high road and been more civilized about it. I knew he was hurting and hoping to be shown some love from me, but what did I do? I kicked him while he was down. I threatened to call the police on him. I used my mouth like a sawed-off shot gun, shooting bullets with the intention to kill. I was like that with everyone, and I needed to stop. It was going to take a lot of self-control, but like Lydia said, harsh and unwise words went hand-and-hand.

"Verse twenty-seven says, 'She looks well to how things go in her household, and the bread of idleness, gossip, discontent, and self-pity, she will not eat.' Wow! I'm not even going to talk about y'all; I'm going to talk about me. Like I told you all before, I had a great job that I had to give up because my family needed me. Every time I wanted to get back into the workforce, something in my family went wrong, and I had to remain at home. I started to feel sorry for myself. I didn't understand why things weren't working out for me. I complained to my friends and family. I complained to my husband. I ate self-pity and discontent. What I didn't realize is that the more I ate of self-pity and discontent, the worse things became for me, the more arguments brewed in my marriage, the more problems my kids seemed to have, the more I began to hate my life. It wasn't until I began to accept my situation and God's will for me and understood that being a wife and mother was a blessing, and then things got better for me.

"As the woman of the house, you set the tone for the household. Your behavior and words will either positively or negatively influence the members of your family. If you are hostile, argumentative, gossipy, discontent, and whatnot, your family will often follow along and replicate that attitude. However, if you are peaceful, joyful, faithful, appreciative, optimistic, kind, and loving, your family will often follow suit. Peace in your home begins and ends with you. If your home is constantly in chaos, before you blame your angry husband or wayward child, first take a look at yourself and assess whether or not you have unintentionally set a negative tone in your household.".

I had to admit that often I allowed myself to wallow in self-pity. Why aren't I married? Why is life so unfair? Why didn't this or that work out? What did I do wrong? Why is this person treating me this way?

I vowed that contentment would be another area of self-improvement. I already had so much to be thankful for so why was I complaining? So many others had it so much worse than me. I was blessed to the tenth power! If I didn't put a pause on the self-pity, I would enter marriage with the same attitude and bring negative energy into my home. I had waited my whole life for a good man who loved me, why should I mess it up by being discontent and feeling sorry for myself? What man wants to be around a complaining woman? Oh, Lydia had me pegged with this class, and all of her words went straight to the heart.

Too bad it would only take a matter of days to forget everything I'd been taught.

Lesson 23: Choose Wisely

And if it seems evil to you to serve the Lord, Chose for yourselves this day whom you will serve, whether the gods which your fathers served on the other side of the River, or the gods of the Amorites, in whose land you dwell; but for me and my house, we will serve the Lord. (Joshua 24:15)

"**M**s. Ross! We have a major problem! You have to come down here now!" Jill, the manager at Sweet Tooth Oasis, hollered into the phone.

I had never heard her sound so unnerved. Jill was one of those people who could be in the middle of a tornado and still talk like she was on the beach sipping pina coladas. That's why she ran my business; there was no crisis too big for Jill to handle…until today. "Calm down, Jill. You can't panic like this. Slow down and tell me what's going on."

She let out a muffled sob. "Please, Ms. Ross. I can't talk right now. It's too…too…big! You've just got to come down here RIGHT NOW!"

"Okay, okay. I'm on my way. I'll be there as soon as I can." I hung up the phone, grabbed, my purse, and darted out the door. Usually, I would tell Eric where I was going in case I had any important calls, but I was so disturbed by Jill's call that I sprinted past him without even saying goodbye. I heard him call out my name, but I didn't have time to indulge him.

A million disastrous thoughts skirted through my mind. Fire? Burglary? Irate customer? Irate employee? Equipment failure? Health Inspector? Murder? Suicide? Bomb threat? Hostage situation?

I was losing it. My heart was beating so intensely I thought it might rip through my shirt. As I drove to the bakery, I started to pray out loud just to stop myself from ruminating about all the "what ifs."

"Please God. I don't know what is going on with my business, but give me peace. Whatever it is, help us get through this, help me know how to handle it. Don't let the enemy steal the blessing that You've given me."

I pulled into the parking lot of Sweet Tooth Oasis and looked around. Nothing appeared out of place. The building was still standing. There were no police surrounding the place, no yellow crime scene tape, no firefighters hosing it down, no ambulance carting away a body. *That's a relief.* Whatever the issue was, it wasn't life threatening.

Still worried, I leaped out of my truck and darted into the store. The first thing I noticed was the rose petals. Hundreds of red rose petals blanketed the floor from the doorway to a table that was normally positioned near the wall, but now it was in the middle of the lobby. I glanced around, feeling like I was in The Twilight Zone. No one was in sight. No Jill, no customers, no employees. "Jill!" I called out, but no response followed.

I was tempted to rush to the back of the store to look for Jill when my eyes were drawn back to the out-of-place table. There was a sheet cake on top of the table, but I was too far away from it to see the details of the cake. Curiously, I walked over to the cake, my arms falling limp as I examined it.

The cake was in the shape of an engagement ring. Below the cake on the gold cardboard that held the cake were the words, "Amber, will you marry me?" written in white frosting. In the middle of the ring cake was a stand with an actual ring box opened revealing a solitaire, princess-cut diamond ring. It had to be at least three carats.

I was so stunned that I didn't hear my employees enter the room or the sound of a man coming up from behind me. I felt hands wrapping around my waist and warm heat in my ear as he asked, "Will you?"

I quickly twirled around to see Jonathan Gold dressed to the nines, smiling at me like he just found out he won the Publisher's Clearinghouse Sweepstakes. He walked past me, picked up the ring box from its stand, and proceeded to get down on one knee.

I could hear Jill and the other employees "oohing" and "ahhing" in the background. Gold removed the ring from the box and took my left hand into his. "Amber, I know we've only been seeing each other for a short time, but I am the kind of man who knows when I have a good thing. I believe in taking risks and going for what I want, and I know you do too. I have no doubt that you are the one for me, so let's not waste any more time. Amber, would you do me the honor of becoming my wife?"

He slid the ring onto my finger before I could say yay or nay. I looked up at my employees who were on pins and needles, waiting for my answer. I could see the envy in Jill's eyes, wishing some man would be so romantic to do all of this for her. I knew how she felt because I had been in her position multiple times. I had watched other women be swept away into wifehood while I sat by idly and wished for my day to come. Finally it was my turn to be the lucky woman with the big ring and the man who adored her. I wasn't sure if Gold was the right man for me, but if I let this opportunity pass me by would I ever get the chance again to be a Mrs.?

I gazed down at Gold who was also ogling me in anticipation. Sighing, I nodded a yes. I guess that was good enough for him because he hopped up and pulled me into a heartfelt hug. Everyone in the building (which was really only about five employees and a customer who came in during the proposal) began clapping and cheering as if this scene was something straight out of a romance movie (I think I watch too many films).

Gold kissed me and hugged me again, excited that he was getting what he wanted. I knew the feeling; I felt the same way when things went my way. I spread my fingers out and stared at the gorgeous ring. Although I wasn't 100 percent sure about the man, I was definitely sure about the ring. The ring made me happy and willing; I smiled in approval of the flawless precious stone. I could tell Gold thought my glee was about him and, I let him have his fairy tale. Why not? With a ring like this, I was most certainly having mine!

I knew I was trifling, but sometimes something mediocre is better than nothing at all. Truth be told, Gold was better than mediocre. I was sporting a three and a half carat ring (yeah, I immediately had it appraised) and my fiancé (love the way that sounded) was worth millions. It might not have been I-can't-live-a-day-without-you love, but it was irrefutably we-can-work-out-the-kinks-later reverence.

Irrespective of my decision to marry Gold, I didn't want to tell Eric. I knew he would be crushed, and I couldn't stand to see him hurting over me. He was a decent man, and he deserved a loving and caring woman. I supposed I just wasn't her.

The next day before I walked into the office, I removed the beautiful ring and concealed it in my wallet. I knew I would eventually have to come clean, but one day into this engagement wasn't the day of full disclosure.

"Amber," Eric yelled out as I tried to hurry past his office.

I was nervous. Did he know already? How would he know? I hadn't told anyone including my mom or Tisha. Had Gold called the office flaunting his victory? With Gold, anything was possible.

I turned back toward his office, plastered a phony smile on my face and replied, "Hey Eric! What's up?"

He leaned back in his chair. "Nothing much. You ran out of here so fast yesterday, I just wanted to make sure you were okay."

"Oh yeah, that. I'm fine. I just was running late to an appointment. You know how that is."

"I understand. Listen, my sister borrowed my car this morning. Hers broke down, and she has the kids and all. I was wondering if I could catch a ride home with you this evening. And if you already don't have plans, maybe we could grab a bite to eat, my treat."

I wanted to say no. Not because I didn't enjoy hanging around Eric, but because I was now officially off limits. I should have said no, but when I opened my mouth what came out was, "Well…uh…sure."

He gave me that you're-the-best smile that I had grown to cherish. "Great. Thanks a lot."

I nodded weakly. "No problem."

It was a problem, however. I was going to hell in gasoline draws. Why did I accept an invitation to dinner with Eric when I was engaged to Gold? Again, was I truly a glutton for punishment? I really did think so.

During dinner, I was unusually quiet. I sat and ate my seafood pasta, Caesar salad, and breadsticks, trying to figure out the best way to break the news. *Eric, Gold and I are getting married.* No. *Gold proposed to me yesterday, and I accepted.* Uh un. How about the truth? *I'm in my thirties and terrified of becoming a part of the statistic of successful, black women who never marry, so when an equally successful black man proposed, I accepted because this chance may never come around again. Sorry.*

Periodically, I would open my mouth to confess and chickened out by saying something irrelevant like, "How's your steak?" or "I hear Nicky (one of our real estate agents) is having another baby." I was such a coward.

By the time I pulled up to his apartment complex, I still hadn't found the nerve to disappoint him. I knew it was selfish of me, but I valued his friendship and wasn't sure he would remain friends or even an employee of mine if he knew the real deal.

"Thanks for the ride and accompanying me to dinner," he said as he unbuckled his seatbelt.

"Anytime." I looked away from him out the driver side window, unable to make eye contact with him because of my guilt.

He didn't get out the car as I hoped. I could feel him watching me. "You seem different tonight. What's up, Amber? You can talk to me; we're friends. Is it your folks again?"

"It's...I...Yeah, I'm still trying to get used to having house guests. It's nothing major." It was the perfect opportunity to confess, but I just couldn't bring myself to it.

"Come here," he whispered, and before it registered to me what was happening, he put his index finger underneath my chin, turned my face towards him, and kissed me softly on the lips. My body shuddered, and I thought to myself, *Great! Now, the fireworks show up!*

He pulled back from me and let out a low groan. "Mmmm. That was amazing. I've wanted to do that for a while now...Just be patient with your mom. Things will work themselves out. Call me if you need me." He flashed me his award-winning smile and exited the vehicle.

Being greedy and lying was what caused people to end up on drama-filled talk shows like Jerry Springer and Maury. One little lie or withholding the truth turns into a huge nightmare that takes daytime TV to unravel. Technically, I just cheated on Gold. Kissing another man is undoubtedly infidelity. We weren't even married yet, better yet, we only got engaged yesterday, and I was already falling into temptation. Yes, Eric kissed me, but I didn't stop him. Frankly, I led him on by going out to dinner with him and not telling him about Gold. It was one thing when there was no allegiance involved, but the ring sparkling in the change compartment of my wallet signified the ultimate commitment.

I dug into my purse and took the ring out of its hiding place and slipped it once again back on my hand. As I headed home, I gazed at the ring at each stop sign and every traffic light. Kissing Eric felt good; it was actually lovelier than kissing Gold, which I had also just experienced for the first time yesterday at the proposal. Was I making a mistake? Was Eric really the one?

I shook my head and fought the silly notions. There was no way that I could back out on Gold now, and Eric didn't come with any guarantees. What if I left Gold to be with Eric, and Eric decided he didn't want to marry me? I would be back where I started and I had come way too far to start all over. I had pleaded with God for a husband, and now I had one. Well almost. I would have to be grateful for the good man He had given me and stop expecting something better.

When I walked into the house forty-five minutes later, Mom and Otis were sitting in the living room, eating popcorn and watching *Love Jones. What did they know about the movie Love Jones? They must have taken the DVD from my video stash.*

Plopping down on an empty recliner, I threw my purse down on the floor and exhaled in exhaustion. "Hey," I murmured.

My head began to ache, a clear sign of stress. I absentmindedly placed my left hand on my thumping forehead, exposing the until that moment secret jewelry. My mom gasped in surprise, causing me to yank my hand quickly away from my face and hide it in my lap.

"Amber Denise Ross! Is that an engagement ring on your finger?"

I swore my mom could have worked for the CIA or FBI! Hiding something from her, especially anything to do with a man, was like hiding drugs in a kennel full of trained, narcotics search dogs used by the police.

I sighed, preparing myself for a nag session. "Yes, mother. It is an engagement ring."

Her bottom lip hit the floor (okay, not literally). "Who are you engaged to? When did this happen? And why didn't you tell us anything?"

I rolled my eyes and spoke in monotone. "Jonathan Gold proposed to me yesterday. I was still getting used to the idea. I haven't told anyone."

"Jonathan? What about Eric?"

"What about Eric? Eric is okay. I just dropped him off at home. We had dinner together. He's in good health." My voice dripped in sarcasm.

"Stop being a smarty pants. You know what I am asking you. How does he feel about you being engaged to Jonathan?"

"Mom, I don't know how he feels because I haven't told him."

"Then why did you go out to dinner with him?"

I sucked my teeth. I didn't know why I was taking my problems out on her. I guess it was because I knew she was a safe and easy target. "Because he asked me to. And since you're digging for information you might want to know that he kissed me too, but that wasn't a part of the plan, at least for me it wasn't."

My mother jumped up from the sofa and rushed over to me, snatching my hand out of my lap and inspecting the ring at close proximity. "Amber! You're serious! This ring is real! Gold asked you to marry him, and you went out on a date with Eric? Are you trying to send me to an early grave?"

I tore my hand away from her. "Mom, this is not about you. When I accepted Gold's proposal and then went out with Eric I wasn't plotting your demise, contrary to your belief. I know you are dying to put your two cents in, so go ahead and say what's on your mind. Tell me how I'm such a horrible person."

I must have taken it too far because she glowered at me and stuck her finger in my face. "Oh, no! You're a grown woman! You don't need your momma's advice or approval! Do what you want to do since you know so much, but let me tell you this here, little missy, marriage is not something to be taken lightly. You don't get married because it's convenient for you or you want to wear a man on your arm like a new fur. Marriage is hard, and if you are going to marry someone, do it with someone you are willing to go through some mess with because there will be mess. I'm not going to tell you not to marry Jonathan because he seems like a fine young man, but if you decide to follow through with this, love that man and be true to him. Don't play games. And tell Eric the truth before he finds out and hates you for lying to him. Humph!" My mother stormed off to her room, leaving a wounded me and an annoying Otis behind.

Otis stared at me, contemplating a remark about the situation. That was how he was. He didn't say much; he just sat back and watched. Then when the drama was over, he was famous for throwing fuel on the fire by slipping in a final, unwanted comment. "What?" I asked nastily. "I know you got something to say, too. What?"

He glared at me. "Listen here, little girl. I know I'm not your daddy—"

I cut him off. "You sure aren't. Glad you finally figured that one out."

He let out one of those angry chuckles. "Child, I'm trying not to disrespect you in your own home, but you are pushing me. Now, your momma and I appreciate all that you're doing for us, but you are not going to keep talking to my wife and me like we owe you. We don't owe you squat. All those years we took care of you so you could have something nice for yourself when you grew up, and this is how you treat us now? Your momma is right. Marriage ain't a playground that you can go to and have fun when you feel like it, and then when you're tired you just go on home. You'd better love this man, I mean really love him, cause if not, you'll be right back here by yourself in a year. I promise you that. And if you're marrying that boy because he got money, you'se a fool! Money don't make the man."

I knew he wasn't talking about me? Who did he think he was trying to give me some advice when he was the last person I wanted in my ear? He acted like money was everything when I was growing up, and now, he was trying to pretend like he was so altruistic! *Get out of my face with all of that!*

"That's not what you taught me. You acted like your money made you the king."

He stood up, enraged. "I was the king of my home and my family. And your mom was my queen. That's what you don't seem to get. A wife submits herself to her husband. You think you gonna run your husband? You sure better have a weak man because a real man ain't gonna take it! Jonathan Gold ain't gonna take it! He might be all starry-eyed right now, but when the honeymoon ends, he is gonna demand respect from you, and if you don't check your attitude, you're gonna lose him!"

He shook his head in disappointment at me and disappeared down the hallway. *What did he know anyway?*

Lesson 24: Make Them Proud

Her children rise up and call her blessed (happy, fortunate, and to be envied); and her husband boasts of and praises her, [saying], Many daughters have done virtuously, nobly, and well [with the strength of character that is steadfast in goodness], but you excel them all. (Proverbs 31:28-29)

Attending class on Monday was the only solace I could find. My houseguests and I were barely speaking. And it was my fault. I was wrong for being so callous towards my mother and Otis when they were just trying to help; however, I hated for people to offer advice when I hadn't asked for it. I hated how everyone thought they knew what was best for me better than I did. I hated that God was being so silent instead of shouting out the answers I only wanted from Him alone.

I had yet to tell Tisha about the engagement, but I wasn't worried about her. She would be ecstatic because she believed all the while that it was Gold who was best for me. I wondered what Lydia would have thought about me marrying Gold? I twisted the ring around so that the diamond faced the palm of my hand. Like I said, I was wondering what she would say, but I wasn't ready for a real response.

"As a mother, one of the things I highly enjoy is bragging on my children," Lydia stated to the class. "Of course, I don't do it in a vicious way, but I do love to tell others about the accomplishments of my children. I love them, so when they do something great, I feel proud and want to share my joy with the world. Those of you who are mothers can relate. If you don't have children, I know you've probably felt this way about a friend, significant other, or family member.

"Proverbs 31: 28-29 reads, 'Her children rise up and call her blessed, happy, fortunate, and to be envied; and her husband boasts of and praises her, saying, many daughters have done virtuously, nobly, and well with the strength of character that is steadfast in goodness, but you excel them all.' The virtuous woman has a family that is proud of her. Just as you want to be proud of your children, your children also desire to feel the same way about you. I remember being a child and my mom did something embarrassing, I felt ashamed of her. How I would have loved to have told the other children that my mom was the very best mom!"

Ooh! I could so relate. *Me too, Lydia!* I wanted the same thing, to feel proud of my mom, but I also felt ashamed. I knew this was why we struggled with getting along until this day.

Lydia continued. "When the child of a celebrity meets other people, most times that child is quick to let everyone know that their mother is so-and-so. Why? Because of name association. People treat you differently when they know that you are related to someone important. That child may get certain benefits or privileges not given to the children of ordinary people. Unless that child wants to blend in, he or she will let people know who his or her mother is so that they can also be recognized.

"Verse twenty-eight tells us that this woman is such an awesome mother that her children are letting folk know how they feel about her. 'That's my mother! She is blessed! You should want to be like her!' Not only that, but after the kids finish bragging on her, her husband comes out and starts singing her praises, too."

Lydia scanned our faces and gave us a look that said we had better listen up because the punch line was on the way. "Here's the interesting part. Her husband doesn't say that his wife is fine or hot. He doesn't say she's a good cook or keeps the house clean. He doesn't mention that she still has a Coke bottle shape or flawless skin. No. He says, 'There are a lot of great women out here, but my wife is better than all of them!' Wow! Now that is a compliment. When you have got a husband saying things like that about you, you never have to worry about him cheating or not coming home at night. Insecurity flies out the door because this man just said that no other woman compares to you. What I like about verses 28-31 is that after the woman's character is described in verses 10-27, we are able to see the concluding impact of her behavior in the last four verses. One of the conclusions of the Proverbs 31 woman is that her family is satisfied and appreciative of her because of all that she is. So let me ask you all one, last important question: How do your husbands and children feel about you?"

Lesson 25: Handle Your Affairs Before They Handle You

[Put first things first.] Prepare your work outside and get it ready for yourself in the field; and afterward build your house and establish your home. (Proverbs 24:27)

I should have told Eric. But I didn't.

When Gold walked into Amber Ross Realty that Thursday with a bouquet of flowers, I knew the bottom was about to fall out. At that moment, I wished I had told Eric, but I hadn't, and now the jig was up.

First of all, Eric really didn't know his job description. He was the office manager, but sometimes he moonlighted as office security. When he saw Gold breezing through the office like he owned the place, his first instinct was to shut Gold down.

"Good Afternoon, Mr. Gold. Do you have an appointment?" Eric asked as he blocked Gold's way to my office.

Second, Gold thrived on getting the upper hand. Now that we were engaged, I was sure that he was waiting for the opportunity to gloat in Eric's face. Gold was the winner, and he was determined to let the second runner up see him holding the trophy.

I saw the commotion in the hallway and knew I was cold busted. Hurriedly, I dug the diamond out of my purse and shoved it onto my finger. I had to get out there before Gold said too much, and Eric caught on to the truth.

Gold laughed. "An appointment? I don't need an appointment to see my fiancé."

Eric winced. "Your fiancé? Who's your fiancé?"

I rapidly jumped up and ran past my desk, eager to intercept the conversation.

"Who writes your checks?" Gold asked smugly.

I was past my office door in a matter of milliseconds. I just had to get there before…

Eric peered at Gold as if he was going berserk. "Amber Ross, who else? Wait! Your fiancé is Amber? Yeah right! Amber can't stand you. She would never marry you."

Too late. I tried to spin around and scurry back into my office before either man saw me, but as I began to tip-toe back, Gold spotted me.

"There she is. Amber!" Gold yelled down the hall at me. I stopped in mid hustle and slowly turned back around to face their direction. Time seemed to drag, as if I was moving in slow motion, or maybe it was actually the pace that I was walking.

Unsure of how to approach the matter, I went into play-it-off mode. "Gold! Hey! What-What are you doing here?"

Gold handed me the floral bouquet and kissed me on the cheek. "Just stopped by to surprise you. You must not have told your assistant about the engagement."

Eric's eyes widened as he studied my face. "Amber, what's going on? You're not marrying him, are you?"

"Of course, she is. You must be blind. Haven't you seen this flawless diamond ring on her finger? She's been wearing it for a week now!" Gold reveled.

Eric's eyes quickly darted to my jewel adorned hand. I followed his gaze down to my ring. The diamond had a certain shimmer to it, but in the heat of the moment, it seemed to sparkle brighter than normal.

I was at a loss for words. Eric's face crumpled like a sundried raisin. "Eric, I…"

Eric looked away and shook his head in defeat. "No explanation is necessary Ms. Ross. I think I've got the picture. Congratulations." He walked into his office. I thought the worst was over, but less than sixty seconds later, he walked back out with his jacket on and a few of his personal belongings in a plastic grocery bag.

"Eric! Eric!" I yelled after him as he brushed past me and Gold, and fled out the front door.

Gold placed his hand on the curve of my back. "Let him go. We can find you another assistant."

I glared at him and shoved the flowers back into his hands. "He's not an assistant, Gold!" Running as fast as my feet in three and a half inch heels could take me, I cornered Eric as he dumped the plastic bag into the trunk of his car.

"Eric! Eric where are you going?" It was a stupid question, but I had to say something.

He slammed the trunk closed, refusing to look at me. "I quit."

What I feared was happening, and I couldn't stop it. Not only was he mad at me and our friendship terminated, but he was also quitting his job. I couldn't let him lose everything; I couldn't lose everything. "You can't just quit. What about a two week notice? This isn't very professional."

"Professional? Are you serious? That's the pot calling the kettle black, don't you think? It's not professional to date both your employee and your business partner at the same time, but I guess you did it anyway! And two week notice? How about you notice for two weeks that I'm not here?" he growled as he unlocked his car door and got in.

It was late, too late, but I had to make him understand. I stepped between the car door and him so that he couldn't shut the door and walk out of my life forever. "I am so sorry if I hurt you. Gold asked me and I said yes, but I don't love him. Believe me, I don't love him."

He frowned at me. Unconvinced, he asked, "So what? Are you saying you love me? Because a woman who loves me wouldn't be marrying another man!"

Tears began to run down my face. It wasn't manipulation; I really felt my emotions overpowering me. "I don't know what I feel when it comes to you. I know I really care about you a lot, and I love being your friend. I just don't know, but I don't want to lose you. I do know that."

I looked in his eyes and saw pure disgust. It pained me awfully for him to stare at me that way. Feeling his disdain, I backed away from his car.

Noticing I was no longer obstructing his path, he grabbed the handle to the car door. "Grow up, Amber! The world does not revolve around you. Other people have wants and needs too. I wanted to be with you. I wanted to build a life with you, but you are too self-centered and controlling and fearful to see a good man when he is standing right in front of you. Instead, you would rather marry a man that you abhor. Why Amber? Because he's rich? Because it's easier to be with someone that doesn't challenge you than to be vulnerable? Stop wasting my time! I thought you were different. I see now that I was so wrong about you!" He banged the car door shut, started the car, and drove away.

"Eric! Eric!" I cried out, but my cries were useless. He was gone.

Lesson 26: Produce What Lasts

Charm and grace are deceptive, and beauty is vain [because it is not lasting], but a woman who reverently and worshipfully fears the Lord, she shall be praised! Give her the fruit of her hands, and let her own works praise her in the gates [of the city]!

(Proverbs 31:30-31)

"Last week we talked about verses 28 and 29, and how they are the beginning of the conclusion of this biblical chapter on the virtuous woman. Today we will examine verses 30 and 31 which are the last two verses of Proverbs 31. These last two verses are the end of the conclusion of the matter," said Lydia.

I was emotionally empty. I thought getting engaged would be the happiest moment of my life, but somehow it seemed to be one of the lowest. Gold was the only person who appeared to be smiling, but I surly wasn't. I had attempted to call Eric several times, but he wasn't picking up or returning my messages. A temp was at the office, filling in until I found another office manager, but I wasn't ready to put out a job announcement. I was praying that he would come back although I knew that the possibility was that this prayer would be in vain.

I couldn't fathom how I could go from having no man to three men to one man who probably wasn't the right man. It was now obvious to me that I was my biggest problem. All the years I spent as a single woman had a lot to do with me and my lack of preparedness for a real relationship, not to mention my fears. God knew to keep me away from good men because I would make a mess, just like I was currently doing. After eleven weeks of Wife 101, I was still as ignorant as the day I began.

I continued to debate the Green Global issue. Perkins, Gold, and I were scheduled to meet in two weeks to look over the final contract. I had until then to make my decision. If I was going to be Gold's wife, I would have to sign the deal. I couldn't start a marriage going against my husband. I knew if I refused to move forward with the deal, my refusal would drastically impact my engagement to Gold. The whole situation added another layer of stress to the entire ordeal.

With the tension still thick at my house, my mom and Otis kept their distance. I tried to work late hours so that I wouldn't cross paths with them too much. With everything that was going on, arguing with them was not an option or a desire. I was overwhelmed and barely made it to class. There were only two more lessons, and I wanted to finish what I had started.

Lydia picked up her bible and licked her index finger before flipping the pages. "Verse thirty reads, 'Charm and grace are deceptive, and beauty is vain because it is not lasting, but a woman who reverently and worshipfully fears the Lord, she shall be praised.' It is amazing that the world encourages us to focus on the main things that the bible says are least important.

"Charm and grace are deceptive. Many people will tell you that if you walk a certain way or use certain words around men, that will hook a man. Maybe if you eat a certain way or bat your eyes and smile, that will get him. The bible, however, says that charm and grace are deceptive. Have you ever met someone who seemed really nice and sweet and innocent, someone who acted very classy, but then when you got to really know them, you realized that their sweetness was all a front? They were really evil or annoying or just not someone you wanted to associate with? Charm and grace are deceptive."

I was pretty sure that was exactly how Eric was feeling about me. I had charmed my way into his life, but when the smoke cleared, an obnoxious version of me was what stood before him.

"Beauty is vain because it is not lasting. Do you remember the most popular girl back in high school or college? You know the one who was so pretty that all the guys wanted to be with her? What is she doing now? What does she look like? Is she still 'All that?' Beauty fades. People gain weight, lose weight, get old, have babies, get sick, hair falls out, hair gets gray, use drugs, all types of things that change their appearance. Imagine marrying someone based solely on his good looks. Good luck with that! Beauty does not last."

Yeah, I was cute, some men even called me fine, but there would always be someone younger, prettier, sexier to contend with. I pondered if Gold liked me for my looks and if he would eventually trade me in for a more beautiful model.

"But a woman who with respect and with worship fears God, she will be lifted up. The key to the life of the virtuous woman is her love, respect, and honor of God. She understands that God is all that she needs to be the best mother, wife, and woman that she can be. No matter what she is going through, God is her focus. She refuses to look away from God, not for anything or any reason, and because of her loyalty, she is praised, she is adored and put on a pedestal."

Therein was my dilemma. I struggled with self-reliance. If I could only learn to depend on God and keep Him as my focus, maybe I would make better choices, maybe I would treat people better, maybe I wouldn't feel so bad. Had God been giving me the answer all the while and I had not been listening? Was it my own voice and the opinions of others drowning out the still small voice of the great I Am? Had I always known the truth of how this thing would turn out but refused to change because it would mean letting go and letting God?

"Finally, Proverbs 31:31 says, 'Give her the fruit of her hands, and let her own works praise her in the gates of the city.' The virtuous woman does not have to talk about how she is this and that; her reputation precedes her. She is fruitful, she is successful. What she does is noticed by others and her impact spreads throughout her neighborhood, city, region, country, or even the world. People come to her and say, 'Hey, aren't you so-and-so? Didn't you do this-and-that?' It's funny how many people think that they have to tell others what they have done. If you have to tell random people what you have done, your works are not praising you. Stop telling people who you are and live your life in a way that your works speak for you. Ask yourself, what does my life say about me?"

My life was screaming that I was one of the most successful failures in the world. There were some things that I could not change. Like the Serenity Prayer, I would have to learn to accept those things and let God ultimately decide the end result. But there were other things that I did have the power to correct, and it was time to take responsibility for those things and make the necessary modifications. Like the old saying goes, sometimes things have to get worse before they can get better, and that was exactly what happened next.

Lesson 27: Forgive and Let Go

For if you forgive people of their trespasses [their reckless and willful sins, leaving them, letting them go, and giving up resentment], your heavenly Father will also forgive you. Matthew 6:14

"Amber! Amber! Wake up! Oh Lord! Amber!" I was yanked from a deep state of sleep by the screeching sound of my mother's frantic voice.

Groggily, I looked at the alarm clock, the blaring red numbers that formed 4:32 a.m. slowly coming into focus. My mother was standing over my bed, shouting and shaking my body. "I'm up! What's wrong?" I managed to murmur.

"It's Otis! I think he's had a heart attack!" she cried. "Oh Jesus! In the name of Jesus!"

I shot up from my bed. "What? Did you call 911?"

"Yes! They're on the way! Come help me!" Satisfied that she had gotten me moving, she dashed out of my room and down the hallway back towards hers. Forgetting a bra and socks, I threw on a pair of blue sweatpants, a green t-shirt, and my sneakers on, and ran down the hallway after her.

Otis was leaned over the side of the bed, holding his chest in pain. My mother was hugging him and praying over him as if he would miraculously jump up and say, "I'm healed!"

I ran over to them and began to peel her body away from his. "Mom! We've gotta get him downstairs so when the paramedics get here it will be easy for them to take him to the hospital."

She held on tighter. "I don't know, Amber! Maybe we shouldn't move him!"

"I don't know either, Mom! I've never dealt with a heart attack before. I think we are supposed to raise his arm above his heart! No! That might be for bleeding! I don't know!" I threw my hands up in complete confusion.

I heard sirens approaching the house and let out a sigh of relief. If left under my and my mother's care, Otis would be a goner. I leapt up and ran down the stairs to usher them in. By the time the paramedics put Otis on a gurney and rolled him out of the house, both my mother and I looked as if we might have needed a hospital bed alongside of his.

My mom hopped into the ambulance and rode with Otis to Crawford Long Hospital while I grabbed my purse and jacket and got into my truck to drive to the hospital. My nerves were in an uproar, causing my hands to jitter so much that by the time I got to the stop sign at the corner, it was evident that I could not drive myself anywhere. I tried to call Gold, but his voicemail picked up immediately, letting me know his phone was off. I left a message telling him what happened and where to find me.

God, if I ever needed You, I really need You right now! I can't do this alone!

I called Tisha who also didn't answer the phone, so I ended up leaving her a message as well. The only other person I could think of who might have come out to support me was Eric, but I knew it was a long shot.

Putting my pride aside, I called him anyway, expecting to be also greeted by his voicemail. Surprisingly he answered with a voice that mimicked mine thirty minutes prior. "Hello?"

"Eric! Oh thank God! Please don't hang up on me! Please!" I cried.

"Amber? Is that you? It's 5 o'clock in the morning. What's going on? Did something happen?"

"Yes! Otis had a heart attack! They're taking him to Crawford Long now!"

"Oh, no! Where are you?"

"I'm in my truck at the corner of my street. I was trying to drive there, but I'm shaking so much that I'm scared I'll end up in an accident."

"Turn around and go back home."

"What?"

"Go home, Amber. I will come pick you up from your house. You can't drive like that. Trust me and go home."

"Okay, okay," I sobbed.

I went back to the house as he instructed. I stayed in my SUV, waiting for him to get there and whisk me away to the hospital. I was concerned that my mother would notice that I didn't get there right away and start to worry about me, too. With trembling hands, I called the hospital's emergency room and had them give her the message that I was okay and waiting on Eric. After hanging up, I wondered how crazy that message must have sounded when they repeated it to my mother. When I showed up at the hospital with him, I would find out for myself.

It took Eric approximately thirty minutes to get to my house. As I waited, I thought about Otis and how awful I had been to him. Not just since they had been staying in my house, but throughout his entire marriage to my mother. If he died today, and I never got to speak to him again, I would have to live with so many regrets for not being kinder to him or even giving him a chance. Technically, he never did anything bad to me. He married a woman who was a widow and a single mom with a bratty kid (me). He took on the fathering role of a child who wasn't his own (me). He may not have always handled every situation the way I thought was best in our home, but he did the best that he knew how and remained faithful to his promise to my mother and to God. I would be lucky to have a man like Otis. I was lucky to have a stepfather like him.

Lord, I've been so wrong about everything! I keep making mistake after mistake. I want to do what is right in Your sight, but somehow I keep doing the opposite of what I should do. Please take over and change me! Help me to let go of the things that are not like You. Otis is a good man. Please give me a chance to tell him that I was wrong. Save Otis, God! Heal him, please!

When I saw Eric pull up into the driveway in his Impala, I finally got out of my truck and climbed into his vehicle, clutching my purse as if I had just robbed a bank and the money was inside it.

I knew I looked a mess. My hair had to be all over my head because I was a wild sleeper and didn't comb or brush it before I left the house. I had morning breath, wearing clothes that didn't match, and probably had sleep in my eyes too. It really didn't matter because Eric more than likely didn't want me anymore. What was it that Lydia said about beauty being vain because it wasn't lasting? Case and point.

"How you holding up?" Eric asked as he cruised out of my driveway and headed toward the hospital.

I looked over at him apologetically. "Still pretty shook up. It just all happened so fast."

He kept his eyes on the road. "Yeah. That's how these things are. My father had a heart attack a few years back. Scared the living daylights out of me too, but it's going to be alright. They're going to take good care of him. God is in control."

"Yeah, He is," I muttered as I turned my head and gazed out of the window. Eric. I had chosen Gold over Eric and look who was here for me when I really needed someone the most. Not Gold, but Eric. Despite all of my rationalizations about why Eric and I wouldn't work out as a couple, I knew he was really the right one for me. Too bad my moment of epiphany occurred a little too late. Although he was helping me out, I could tell by the seriousness in his face, the way he gripped the steering wheel, and the fact that he hadn't made eye contact with me the whole time we had been in the car that he had made his decision to leave me alone for good. All the good adages were mocking me. You never miss your water till your well runs dry. Hindsight is 20/20. It's a thin line between love and hate. Well, maybe not the last one, but you get the picture.

We got to the hospital in record time and found my mother sitting in the emergency room rocking back and forth and praying.

"Mom! Have you heard anything?"

"They had to take him into emergency surgery. You know I don't understand all that medical jargon. I called your brother and told him. He wanted to come but I told him, not yet. Let's see what they say first. Oh Amber! What am I going to do without my Ottie?"

Ottie? My mom really did love this man, and I had made her pay for it. "Mom, he's not going anywhere. It's going to be okay." I rubbed her forearm, praying I was right.

My mom finally noticed Eric standing behind me and smiled. "Thanks for coming, Eric."

"I wouldn't dream of being anywhere else," he replied compassionately.

My mom's eyes shifted back to me, and I instantly knew what she was thinking. I nodded my head to let her know she was right. I should have chosen Eric.

Eric…Gold? Bah, Humbug!

The surgery was successful. My mother, Eric, and I sat by Otis' bed and watched him as he calmly rested. We had called my brother and told him the good news. Of course, he was relieved to know his father was okay. It was now going on 9:00 a.m., and I wondered how much longer Eric would stay. I planned to take the day off and be there for my mom, but Eric could go when he pleased.

At 9:12 a.m. Tisha burst into the room. "Oh, Anita! Is he okay?" she whispered loudly as she swept past me to the arms of my mother.

My mother gave her a long, loving hug. "Yes. God is good. The doctor says he's gonna be fine."

Tisha placed her hand on her chest and let out a heavy sigh. "Thank you, Lord!" She then turned to me and said, "Girl, I'm so sorry. I got your message a couple hours ago, but you know I had to go to the school and make sure everything was in order for the day before I came here. But you knew I was coming, right?"

I smiled, glad that she was dependable. "Yeah, I knew you'd be here…eventually."

She peered at Eric. I knew she didn't care much for him, but at least he answered the phone in the middle of the night. "Mm Hmm," she replied. "Hi, Eric."

I was sure he could feel her lack of acceptance. "Hello, Tisha," he returned.

Tisha looked down at my hand and noticed the sparklingly jewel. She gave me a what-the-devil look and moaned a disapproving, "Mmm Mmm."

I knew she thought I was engaged to Eric instead of Gold. I had yet to tell her the story, which she was going to kill me for because we were supposed to be best friends. What woman doesn't tell her best friend the moment after the question is popped? Me.

"Eric, if you have something to do I can catch a ride home with Tisha. I mean, it's fine if you want to stay, but I don't want to hold you up. You've been so wonderful tonight. Thank you so very much."

Eric stood, walked over to my mom, and gave her a tight, comforting hug. Just as he was releasing her, Gold barged into the room looking like he stepped off the front page of *Black Enterprise* magazine. No wonder he was the last to arrive. It probably took him three hours to get dressed.

"Amber, I didn't get your message until an hour ago. How is he?" Gold inquired.

Eric stood straight up and critically eyed Gold, who noticed Eric and let out an arrogant grunt. I bit my lip, praying that no drama would "pop off" in my stepfather's hospital room. Tisha glanced excitely back and forth between the two men. She was always good for sniffing out tension. My mom looked at me and poked out her lips as if to say, "Handle your business!"

I quickly stood up. "Hey, Gold. Otis is hanging in there. He had surgery, but everything went well. Excuse me while I walk Eric out."

I grabbed Eric's hand and led him out the door. *Whew! That was close!*

We stepped into the hallway and I closed the door behind us. "I'm sorry about that," I offered.

He shrugged. "It's cool. I mean, he is your fiancé. He should be here with you and your family."

"Eric, I really want to explain to you—"

He held up his hand to silence me. "Save it, Amber. Please tell your stepfather that he's in my prayers." Eric pulled his keys out of his jacket pocket and strolled down the hallway towards the parking garage.

I felt like crying, but it wasn't the time. Pulling myself together, I reentered the room where all eyes fell on me. Gold was sneering at me so I knew he was the next person in line that I had to deal with.

"Gold," I called out to him and motioned my head for him to follow me outside.

The door barely closed behind us before he started grilling me. "Amber, what are you doing? Why is it that every time I turn around, you are running after Eric?"

I almost snapped. "For your information, when I couldn't reach you or anyone else, Eric was the one who answered his phone, Eric was the one who got out of his bed in the middle of the night, and Eric was the one who drove me to the hospital so that I could be here for my mother and stepfather. You are my fiancé, and you are just showing up five hours later. So don't even go there."

Seeming stung, Gold backed up slightly. "I'm sorry. I saw him and got paranoid. I'm glad he was able to help you. Are you okay?"

I ran my finger through my untamed hair. "Yeah. It's been a crazy night. You go ahead on to work, and Tisha's going to take me home so I can take a shower and change my clothes."

"Are you sure? I don't mind taking you."

"No, no, but thanks. And thanks for coming." I kissed him on the cheek and watched him walk away before I proceeded back into the room.

Once again, all eyes were on me (except Otis', of course). "Mom, I'm going to have Tisha take me to the house to change my clothes and get my truck. Do you want to go with us or me to bring you anything back? I should be back in an hour or two."

"No, you go. And you don't have to rush back. Take your time. Get a nap. I know you have to be exhausted. Just bring me a change of clothes and I can wash up in the bathroom over there. I want to make sure I'm here when he wakes."

"I understand." I walked over to her and gave her a tight hug. "I love you," I whispered into her ear before I let go. She smiled and nodded, her way of saying she loved me, too.

The moment I slid into Tisha's BMW, she looked over at me and said in a horrible Spanish accent, "Lucy, you got some splainin' to do!"

I laughed. "I know, you're going to kill me." I told her everything, from the situation with Chris, to Gold's engagement, to Eric's quitting. I even told her about the friction between my parents and me. As much as Tisha can be opinionated and difficult at times, it felt good to vent and get it all off my chest.

"I can't believe I'm just finding out about all of this now! Let me see this ring!" She lifted my hand with her free hand that wasn't on the steering wheel and took a quick look at the ring before turning her attention back to the road. "Wow! That's a nice ring!"

I spread my fingers out and admired it. "Yeah, it is gorgeous."

Tisha squealed. "I can't believe you're getting married! So I know I'm the maid of honor!"

"Of course, but…"

She gasped. "You got someone else in mind? I've been your friend and put up with your shenanigans for way too long to not be your maid of honor!"

She was so dramatic! I waved my hand to calm her down. "No. I mean, yes you will be my maid of honor. There is no one else I would consider other than you. I was saying that I don't know if I should marry Gold. I think I made a mistake. I know you don't like Eric, but I think he would make a better husband."

She sucked her teeth. "Girl, wake up and smell the coffee! Yes, Eric's a good guy, but Gold is the one who proposed, not Eric. Are you willing to risk a sure thing for something that may never be?"

"Mm. Good question. Good question."

Back home I showered and dressed in a clean pair of sweatpants and matching sweatshirt. My intention was to head straight back to the hospital, but hunger and fatigue started to take over. I slid a frozen pizza into the oven and watched my favorite movie, *Imitation of Life* until the pizza was ready. After eating a few slices, I lay on the sofa and drifted off to sleep for a couple of hours.

When I awoke, it was after 1:00 p.m. I went to my mom's room and stuffed a pair of jeans, a long sleeved shirt, and some clean underwear into an overnight bag.

Father God, please continue to heal Otis. Give my mother peace and let her rest in Your loving embrace. Help me to be obedient to You and to love and forgive as You have loved and forgiven me.

By 1:30, I was in my truck driving back to the hospital.

Opening the door to Otis' hospital room, I saw my mom talking to him. He was now awake, but he was obviously tired and heavily medicated. I passed my mom the bag of clothes and sat down next to her in one of the empty bedside chairs. After fifteen minutes, she decided to run down to the cafeteria and pick up a sandwich to eat. I agreed to stay with Otis while she ate and changed her clothes.

When she left the room, I stood up and walked over to Otis' bed. It may not have been the best moment to deal with our issues, but after last night's scare, I refused to prolong it anymore.

"Otis, I am really sorry for how I've treated you over the past twenty-five or so years. When you married my mother, I guess I was worried that you were going to take the place of my father. My mom loved you so much that it was almost like my real dad never existed. You were so different than my daddy, and I didn't understand your ways so I gave you a hard time. Last night I realized that you weren't the enemy; I was being my own enemy. You came into our lives and gave us another chance to have a whole family. I want you to know that I appreciate all that you've done, I forgive you for anything that you unintentionally did to hurt me and I receive your forgiveness for the things I did to hurt you." I laughed. "It's probably best that you can't do much talking right now so that I could get this all out. You're a good man, and I hope that the man I marry loves me and accepts me the way you've loved and accepted my mother and me."

Otis attempted a small smile and mumbled, "Thank you." A tear rolled out of the crevice of his right eye and fell onto the white pillow below. I sniffled back my tears, not wanting this to become a big, emotional to do. Inside, I felt at peace for the first time in weeks. I had a feeling that this whole ordeal was a part of God's answer to me. I needed to resolve my problems with my stepfather and mother if I wanted to move forward with my life. I hated that Otis had to suffer a heart attack just for me to finally see my faults, but God surely knew how to get my attention.

I squeezed his hand and said the four words I had never said to him, but I knew he'd always wanted to hear: "I love you, Dad."

I got home that evening around 8:30. My mother had decided to spend the night at the hospital with Otis so I'd left her there, promising to bring breakfast and more clothes in the morning. Sitting in my empty house, I felt a nudge in my spirit that I couldn't explain. Chris' name kept flashing through my mind as if I should reach out to him. At first, I ignored the feeling as if I was just tripping, but when the impulse wouldn't recede, I gave in and picked up the phone to call him.

"Amber?" he answered, apparently surprised that I was calling.

"Yeah. Hi, Chris. How are you?"

"I'm here. How about you?"

"I'm here, too. Actually, it's been a hectic twenty-four hours, but it's turned out well."

"Did something happen?"

"My stepfather had a heart attack early this morning. We had to rush him to the hospital and he had surgery. But he is doing okay, thank God."

"I'm sorry to hear that. Is there anything that I can do?"

"No, but thanks for asking. Listen, I called you because I need to say something to you. I know I have been mean to you, and I was wrong for that. When you disappeared on me and proposed to another woman, you really broke my heart. I wanted to give us another chance because I still had feelings for you, but I've realized that I am not the woman for you. You loved Noel, not me. I know she has some issues to work out, but running back to me is not the solution. You need to find a woman that you really want to spend your life with. You never felt that way about me, I was just comfortable. That's why you never proposed to me. A man knows when he meets the right one. Unfortunately, I wasn't her for you.

"I hope that you can deal with what's going on and not use women or alcohol as a Band Aid for the pain that you feel. You will only find yourself in deeper problems than you began with. And I want you to know that I no longer hold our breakup against you. You're forgiven by both me and God. So basically I want to know…can we be friends again?"

The line was quiet, so quiet that I thought I'd lost him. "Chris?"

"I'm here. I heard you, I was just…Yeah, we can be friends. I really need a good friend right now, someone I can trust."

We talked for thirty more minutes. He opened up to me about the Noel situation and how it had pushed him into drinking. He said he'd been sober for the past few days and planned to stop drinking all together. He was scared of becoming an alcoholic. I told him about my engagement to Gold. He said he was jealous but congratulated me anyways. By the time our conversation ended, a huge weight had been lifted from me. I had let go of my anger and resentment towards my stepfather and Chris, two of the men who had a profound impact on my outlook and emotions towards men. It felt good to be free of the negativity. I wasn't sure of what would happen next, whether or not I would marry Gold, but I knew God was in control and that whatever happened would be for my good.

Lesson 28: Know A Few Good Recipes

Through skillful and godly Wisdom is a house (a life, a home, a family) built, and by understanding it is established [on a sound and good foundation], And by knowledge shall its chambers [of every area] be filled with all precious and pleasant riches.

Proverbs 24:3-4

Lydia walked across the front of the classroom as if we were preparing to go to war and she was our Commander in Chief. "Ladies, over the past twelve weeks we have studied the chapter of Proverbs 31. Today is our final class, a summation of all that we have reviewed. I am so proud of all of you for sticking in there and finishing the class. I'm not sure if you all have noticed, but not one of you has dropped out. Usually at least one or two people, sometimes more, start a class but never finish, but God has preserved all of you. There are twelve of you like the twelve disciples. Even one of the disciples, Judas, did not make it, but all of you did, and I thank God for that. Okay, I'm rambling now! Please take out your bibles and turn to Proverbs 31."

We followed her orders and pulled out our bibles, flipping them open to the chapter we had devoted the past three months of are life to studying. Being in the final class was both sad and satisfying. I was also proud of myself for not quitting and for maintaining my commitment. I had learned so much along the way and was certain that I was growing in my relationship with Christ, as well as in my understanding of myself.

"We started the course discussing verse 1-9. These verses inform us that King Lemuel's mother imparted words of wisdom upon him, including the importance of his relationship with women. In verse 10, we learned that a virtuous woman is a rarity and is valued above the treasures of this world. In verse 11, we discussed the impact of this woman on her husband, his ability to trust and believe in being connected to her. Verse 12 focused on the idea that she builds her husband up instead of tearing him down. In verse 13, we discussed her being a hard worker and willing to help, build, and create.

"Verse 14 discusses what this woman brings to the marriage, her nontangible assets. Verse 15 highlights her prayer life and willingness to prepare her family for their day. In verse 16, she shows us the importance of prioritizing and not over committing oneself. In 17, we ascertained the need for physical, mental, and spiritual strength.

"Verse 18 shows us that she lets her light continually shine, while verse 19 demonstrates her skillfulness. Verse 20 establishes her giving nature. Verse 21 identifies her job as a preparer for the family. In verse 22, she displays her self-care and love.

"Verse 23 reflects the success of her husband because of who she is, and verse 24 introduces her as a money maker and businesswoman. In verse 25, she wears her dignity and confidence, while in verse 26 we appreciate her kind and wise words.

"Verse 27 points out her contentment. Verse 28 reflects the positive outlook her children have of her while verse 29 tells of her husband's adoration for her. Verse 30 emphasizes godliness over beauty and charm. Finally in verse 31, she is rewarded by the fruit she bears."

"Wow! What a woman! What a role model for the rest of us," Lydia added.

Lydia pulled out a familiar looking letter-size envelope. "In here are your lists that you created during the first week of class. I asked you to write down the qualities and traits you possessed that made you a good woman. I collected them and sealed them in this envelope. Now I am passing them back to you. Look over them and notice what you wrote down as a reflection of your character." She ripped open the envelope and one-by-one passed each of us our original list.

"Now, I will read a list to you based on Proverbs 31 of the qualities of a virtuous woman," she continued. "If you have any of these qualities already written on your paper, put a check mark next to them. If not, do nothing. A virtuous woman is rare, valuable, capable, intelligent, honorable, trustworthy, motivating, comforting, encouraging, merciful, willing, resourceful, hard-working, prepares, prays, does not over obligate herself, prioritizes, conserves, is mentally, physically, and spiritually strong, faithful, illuminating, skillful, giving, protects, covers, practices self-care, positively influences her husband's success, persuasive, a businesswoman, dignified, wise, kind, content, a blessing to her family, authentic, God-fearing, and fruitful."

I followed along and was only able to check off five of her traits that were on my list.

"Out of the forty traits I just listed, how many of them did you originally have on your list? You don't have to speak your answer out loud, but count them up and write the number on your paper." I wrote down the number five, feeling like I had a lot of growing to do.

Lydia began to hand out another sheet. "I am going to pass out a copy of these forty traits of the virtuous woman. I want you to put a check mark next to each quality that you feel you currently exhibit. You may not have had this quality when the class first started, but you may have developed it over the past three months. Or you may find that you had a trait when we started that you no longer possess."

I went through the list and checked off fifteen of the forty traits. I felt a little better, but still far from where I wanted to be.

"I want you to now compare the two numbers. Have your virtuous traits increased or decreased? How so? Also ask yourself which traits don't you currently possess that you aspire to grow in. Put a star next to these qualities. You'll be able to take this list home with you and use it to work on yourself from here on out."

I put a star next to all of the traits that I had not checked. I wanted my life to reflect a life of virtue, and I was willing to work towards it, even if it took the rest of my life. The good thing was that my number increased by ten. Some of the traits I already had but did not account for, and some were ones I had grown into over the past twelve weeks. God was obviously working on me, and He wasn't through yet.

The class ended with a prayer in which each of us rededicated our lives to Christ, our families, and our communities and committed ourselves to growing in the faith. We filled out a short survey, providing feedback to Lydia and the church about the class so that it could be under consideration to be offered again in the future. Finally, we all hugged and encouraged each other as Sisters in Christ should.

Prior to the class, I had decided that I would finally open up to Lydia and talk to her about my situation. She had made herself available to me, but I had been so afraid to be honest with her. I was worried that I would be judged or frowned upon, but after getting to know her for thirteen weeks, I was sure she wasn't the type to criticize. Lydia was full of love and wisdom, both qualities that I really needed from someone who gave me counsel. I wished I had spoken to her before, but late was better than never.

One by one the ladies in the class filed out, many stopping to thank Lydia for her services as they exited the room. I lingered in the classroom, wanting to be the last out the door so that I could get her undivided attention.

"Sister Ross!" she greeted me as I made my way to the front of the class, the last one to go.

It was now or never. I inhaled and held out my hand to shake hers. "Sister Woods. The class has truly been life changing. I know you gave me your phone number months ago and told me to call you if I ever needed to talk. I wanted to use it plenty of times, but my pride got in the way. I know it's a lot to ask with this being the last class, but I would really love a few minutes of your time."

She clasped my hand within hers and released it. "Not a problem. I knew you'd eventually come along. I believe there is a Starbucks down the street. Let's go grab a cup of coffee and chat."

I ordered a Mocha Frappuccino; Lydia ordered a Caramel Macchiato. With our drinks in our hands, we sat down on a comfy pair of club chairs in the corner of the coffeehouse. The easy listening music playing softly in the background helped to smooth out the relaxing ambiance. I was a sucker for coffeehouses and glad that Lydia made the recommendation to talk there.

Lydia removed the plastic cap from her cup and stirred a sugar packet into her beverage. "When I first saw you signing up for the class, I knew one day we would be here. There was something about you. God laid it upon my heart to pray for you and be available to you. I knew He was going to be working overtime in your life." She replaced the cap and looked up at me expectantly. "So tell me, what's been going on?"

I slurped up the frozen drink before responding. "Wow! Really? I was praying a lot, but God seemed so quiet. I felt like He was ignoring me, but I guess He was hearing and answering my prayers the whole time."

"He always hears us. He may not always respond the way we would like, but that doesn't mean He isn't moving on our behalf. He heard you, and He was impressing upon my heart to care for you."

I put my drink down on a wooden side table. "Why didn't you ever say anything to me about what you were sensing about me?"

"I did. I offered you my phone number and gave you opportunities to talk to me. Until today, you never took them. We have to let people come to us when they are ready. Until you were ready to talk to me, there was nothing I could do but pray for you and give you the lessons in class. Many times people overstep their boundaries, forcing themselves on us before we are open to them, causing us to pull away and resist them and what they have to say. Even if it is the truth. If we really want to help people, we have to trust them in the hands of God, intercede for them through prayer, and believe that God will bring them to us when He is ready and has prepared their hearts for the message we have for them."

"Well, I'm definitely ready. It's good to know He had a plan."

"Yes, it is. So speak your mind." She sipped the drink hesitantly indicating that it was still too hot to drink.

I spent the next thirty minutes telling her my story. I told her why I joined the class and about my relationship with Chris. I told her about Eric and Gold and about Chris coming back. I told her about my parents and the engagement and the heart attack. I even told her about Green Global and Tisha and all of the bad advice I had gotten along the way. I also shared about my growing relationship with Christ and how I had recently learned to forgive the men in my life as well as myself.

"Wow! You've had quite a journey!" Lydia said as she finished off the now cooled down coffee.

I laughed. "You can say that again!"

"So what's the next step?"

"I don't know. I'm supposed to marry Gold, but I'm having second thoughts. Do you think it's a bad idea to marry him?"

"What do you think?"

I sighed. That was the million dollar question. "He's a good man, but my heart is not with him. My heart is with Eric who hates me."

She tilted her head curiously. "Do you really believe that Eric hates you? Someone who hates you wouldn't come to your rescue in the middle of the night."

"That's just Eric. He would do it for anyone. He's just a good person like that."

"You think so? I don't know. Most people only make those kinds of sacrifices for people they love."

I frowned skeptically. "I would give anything for Eric to take me back, but I just don't think it's going to happen. And if I can't be with him, then Gold is the next best thing. I know it sounds a little desperate, but I really want to settle down."

Lydia put her empty cup down on the table. "Let me ask you a question. When Chris wanted to be with you because he couldn't be with Noel, how did that make you feel?"

"Like second best."

"So if you didn't want to play second in Chris's heart, why would you make Gold play second in yours?"

I moaned at the truth. "I never thought about it like that. I'm doing the same thing Chris did to me, but we didn't start out like that. When I accepted Gold's proposal, I wasn't sure how I felt about Eric. I didn't know my feelings were so deep."

"But now you do. I'm not going to tell you not to marry Gold. Whatever decision you make, you will have to be the one to live with it, but I will encourage you to pray about it and follow the leading of the Holy Spirit."

"What if I walk away from Gold, and Eric never comes back? What if I never receive another proposal? What if I end up an old maid?"

Lydia reached over and patted my hand which rested on the arm of the chair. "Life with God is not a life that can be controlled by us. It is filled with the what ifs. The one thing that we can rest in is that God knows what is best for us. When we trust Him and submit to His will, we allow Him to gives us the best, what He always had in mind for us. God loves you, and He knows your heart. I know that it is difficult to walk away from something you've always wanted, but if God tells you to wait, trust Him and He will give you more than you ever imagined was possible. Faith is the substance of things hoped for, the evidence of things not seen."

Lesson 29: All That Glitters Isn't Gold

My fruit is better than gold, yes, than refined gold, and my increase than choice silver. I [Wisdom] walk in the way of righteousness (moral and spiritual rectitude in every area and relation), in the midst of the paths of justice, That I may cause those who love me to inherit [true] riches and that I may fill their treasuries.

(Proverbs 8:19-21)

A few days later, I met with Perkins and Gold to review the final contract for the Green Global venture. Our lawyers and their lawyers had finally come up with a negotiation that was suitable for both parties. We didn't get all of our demands met, but the deal was as close as we were going to get. That's business; full of compromises.

As I sat in their Peachtree St. conference room, flipping the pages of the revised contract, I knew I couldn't sign the document. I had been debating the issue over and over again in my mind, never once feeling confident about ignoring my gut reaction to walk away from it all. Although I still felt extremely guilty and obligated, at the same time, I realized that I had a commitment to God to do the right thing and that promise was bigger than the one I had given my potential business partners.

"I've looked over this document several times, and everything looks good." Perkins, voice cut through the silence and my contemplating thoughts. "If everyone is okay with this, I suggest we go ahead and sign it now. I'll have it notarized then FedEx it to Green Global and we will be in business."

"I say let's do this," Gold replied, his pen already in his hand and ready to sign the documents.

"Amber?" Perkins eyed me critically, waiting for me to agree so that we could close the deal.

I released the pages that were suspended in my hand, causing them to fall flat onto the wooden table. It was time to stop delaying the inevitable. "Unfortunately, I maintain my position from our previous meeting. I'm unwilling to move forward with this project. I know we have all put a lot into this partnership, but I cannot sign these documents and retain a clear conscious. I'm sorry."

Perkins looked as if he had just been sucker punched in the jaw. A red tint quickly spread across his face from ear to ear. His upper lip began to quiver. Gold must have also noticed his intense physical reaction because he tried to mediate the situation.

"Amber, baby. I know you feel a certain level of moral responsibility to this matter, and we appreciate that. That's one of the reasons that you are a part of this partnership; you help to balance us out. But let's not be hasty. We have a lot riding on this deal, and we can't afford to lose it all. Come on, baby. Do this for me."

He was laying it on thick, but nothing he said mattered. I cared about him, I even cared about Perkins, and for that reason I could not be involved with something that was destined to crumble. What is done in darkness will eventually be brought to the light.

"I am doing this for you. I'm doing this for the both of you. My mother used to say 'warning comes before destruction.' We have been warned that this is not the type of corporation that we want to become entangled with. We can heed the warning and walk away now, unscathed, or we can foolishly enter into this agreement and watch it blow up in our faces. I'm not going to put everything I have built in jeopardy. However, if you two want to risk it...."

I began packing up my things, leaving the unsigned contract on the table in front of me. I stood up to leave and politely said, "Good day, gentlemen."

"You little tramp!" Perkins jumped up from his seat and lunged at me. I backed up to avoid his grasp. "How could you ruin everything for us? You selfish floozy!" he barked.

Gold ran over to me to protect me from Perkins's rage. "You should get out of here now!" he pleaded. "I'll meet you in the parking lot. Go!"

I quickly exited the room, looking back only once to see Gold attempting to subdue Perkins, blocking his path so that he couldn't chase after me.

I was trembling by the time I made it down the elevator and out the building's front door. I never thought he would get that hostile, that Perkins would attack me and call me names. Normally, I would have been ready to fight, but when it came to business, I believed in preserving my professional composure even in the most drastic scenarios. I also couldn't fault him because I should have backed out of the deal when I first received the investigative report on Green Global. By remaining on the team, I had given Perkins false hope that I would eventually come around to seeing it his way despite the fact that I knew then things would end in this manner.

Gold met me at my car ten minutes later. I could see the disappointment in his face. He really thought I would stand by his side on this one. He really didn't know the real me.

"Amber, you sure have a way with people!" he joked, trying to ease the tension.

I let out a stifled laugh. "I'm starting to notice that."

Gold glanced around the parking lot then fixed his eyes on me, his expression turning serious. "I'm not going to lie. I'm not happy with your decision, and, of course, Perkins is livid. If we're going to be married, I need to know you're going to have my back and support me even if you don't always agree."

"I figured you would feel that way, and I understand." I twirled the ring around my finger then slowly, sadly, removed it from my finger and offered it back to him.

He refused the ring, grimacing in the process. "What are you doing? I didn't say I was breaking things off with you over this. I am only trying to tell you what my expectations are for the future."

"I know what your expectations are. It pains me to do this, but Gold, I can't marry you."

"Why? Because of this deal? Because I want to want to do business with Green Global?" he shouted.

"No, that's not it. I don't love you. I'm not in love with you, and I probably never will be. If I marry you, it will just be for the sake of being married, and that's not what I want and that's not what you deserve. You should be with someone who can't imagine their life without you. I will never feel that way about you."

"Amber, I know our relationship is unorthodox and that we might not be head over heels in love, but it can still work. We're perfect for each other."

I shook my head. "No, we are not. Marriage is a serious step. It is a commitment before God to love, and honor, and respect each other. We've been engaged less than a month, and I've already cheated on you."

His eyes widened. "You had sex with someone else?"

"No. Cheating is not just sex. The bible says that if you commit a sin in your heart it's the same as doing it. I have imagined being married to Eric instead of you. And the day after you proposed, Eric and I kissed."

"I knew he wanted you back!" he exclaimed, "but it's okay. I forgive you. I mean it was just a kiss. He didn't even know you were engaged then."

"But I knew. Yes, he kissed me, but I didn't stop him. I love him. I can't marry you because I love Eric," I admitted.

Hurt filled his eyes. "You're not in love with me, but you're in love with Eric?"

"I'm not in love with either of you, but I do love him in a way that if nurtured will blossom into being in love. I know it. I just have to give us a real chance. He is the kind of man I need. A man who fears God, someone I can be myself around, someone who is my friend and confidant." A tear trickled down the side of my face, and I instantly wiped it away. "At this point, he may not even want me anymore, but I can't marry you as a second choice. My husband has to be my first choice, and I his. I'm really sorry, Gold." I extended my hand again, offering him the ring back. He accepted it this time, folding it deep into his palm.

"Amber," he begged.

I kissed him on his cheek. "Thank you for giving me the hope that marriage is meant for me." Turning away, I got into my SUV and drove away.

Lesson 30: He Knows Your Name Because It's His Own

Then Adam said, This [creature] is now bone of my bones and flesh of my flesh; she shall be called Woman, because she was taken out of man. (Genesis 2:23)

Three weeks passed without any word from Eric. I was hoping that we would have a Lifetime movie ending where I left Gold standing in the parking lot and have Eric waiting at my house for me when I got there. The only people waiting for me when I got home were my mother and my recently released from the hospital stepfather. Eric was nowhere in sight.

I went to work each day hoping that he would come by the office wanting his job back or even better, wanting me back, but his return did not happen. I continued to avoid hiring someone to replace him, utilizing the temp service to fill in the gap. Not having a fulltime office manager meant I had to take on a lot of the work that was going undone, meaning longer hours for me, but I accepted the extra work gladly. Working was better than sitting around trapped by my memories and regrets. The Wife 101 course had ended, leaving another space in my life that used to fill my Monday nights. My world seemed empty. Gold and I weren't speaking, and Chris was trying to get his life back together. I hung out with Tisha on the weekends, but nothing I did, not shopping or working or even sleeping could take away the ache inside my heart. I missed Eric so much I hurt, but I felt there was nothing I could do about it.

I awakened Saturday morning to the smell of frying bacon, homemade French toast, scrambled eggs, grits, and sausage. Pulling my robe on, I descended downstairs to see who was cooking and if they were making enough for me. I was a little down, but not sad enough to quit eating. I still believed in good food, and my appetite was in full working order.

When I walked into the kitchen, Momma was hovered over the stove, flipping French toast. Deviously, I hugged her from behind, trying to bribe her with my affection. "Morning, Mom. Mmm! That looks delicious."

She chuckled and turned off the pot of boiling grits. "I see someone hasn't lost her appetite." She took a ceramic plate out of the cabinet and fixed me a plate with a little bit of everything on it. I sat down at the kitchen table with a fork and a knife ready to dig in as she set the plate before me and passed me the syrup.

"So, when are you going to open up and talk about it?" she asked curiously as she took the seat across from me.

"Talk about what?" I feigned ignorance.

"Don't play stupid with me, child! You stopped wearing that man's ring weeks ago, and you've been sulking around this house ever since." She got up from the table and removed the French toast that was cooking from the pan, turning the stove off simultaneously.

I forked a piece of sausage into my mouth and chewed. I'd wondered how long she would go before intruding into my business. She was never able to mind her own. "I broke things off with Gold. We're not getting married or even dating anymore. Nothing in particular happened between us; he is just not the man for me."

She watched me closely as she reclaimed her seat at the kitchen table. "Hmm. So, who is the man for you?"

"I don't know."

"I think you do."

I dropped my fork onto the plate. It clattered as it connected with the hard surface. "You want me to say that Eric is the right man for me, don't you?"

She sat back and folded her arms. "I want you to be honest with me and yourself and speak the truth."

"He doesn't want me anymore."

"Say it."

"It's too late."

"Say it."

"He won't answer my calls."

"Say it."

I beat my fist against the table. "Okay! Eric is the man for me! He is the one and I've been blind and a fool! You were right! You warned me and I didn't listen! Are you happy?"

She smiled. "Are you?"

"No! I'm not happy. I miss him so much," I began to sob.

"Then what are you going to do about it?"

I sniffled. "There's nothing I can do!"

She reached over and caressed the side of my face with the back of her hand. "There is always something you can do. You can always pray."

"I'm the one who messed up! How can I pray about it now?"

She got up and extracted a tissue from the tissue box on the counter and handed it to me. "Do you think God didn't know you were going to screw this thing up before he put Eric in your path? God is sovereign. Your steps are ordered. He knew what you were going to do before you did it, and most importantly, He even knows how to untangle you from the chaos that He knew you were going to create. You simply have to believe that He is greater than all of your problems and that there is nothing too hard for Him.

"Don't let your pride keep you from His mercy and grace. You don't have to bear the weight alone." She stood behind me and gently massaged my shoulders. "You've always been so independent, but God didn't make us to be islands. The beauty and blessing is in collaboration. God promises that if two people touch and agree, that prayer will not go unanswered. I'm willing to touch and agree with you, I'll pray with you right now, but you have to take the lead."

I turned around in my seat towards her, and she kneeled down next to me on the rug that extended from underneath the table. I wiped my face with the tissue and balled it up in my hand. She was right. I was still trying to understand it with my own thinking versus believing God could set things straight. If there was any hope, it was in God, not in myself or Eric. I gripped my mother's hands and bowed my head to pray.

"Heavenly Father, I know I have made a lot of bad decisions and that I don't deserve Your grace, but You give it to me despite my faults, and I thank You for being faithful to me even when I'm not to You. Please forgive me. I made a bad choice and hurt someone I truly love. I know if anyone can mend this broken relationship, it is You. I ask that You help Eric to forgive me and if it is Your will for us to be together that You remove every obstacle that stands in the way. In Jesus name, Amen."

My mother stood up and hugged me, reflecting the love that God had for me, filling me with the assurance that everything would be okay.

Two days later I was driving to meet with a real estate client who wanted to view a house out in Covington, GA. I usually did not meet with clients anymore (that's what I paid my agents to do), but the assigned agent was on maternity leave, and Eric, the one who normally stepped in on these occasions, was no longer an employee of Amber Ross Realty. Just as I came close to exit 88 on I-20 East, the first exit in the city of Covington, the client called me saying their car wouldn't start and they would need to reschedule.

"Excellent!" I yelled out sarcastically after I hung up the phone. I exited the highway, looped around, and got right back on the interstate, this time going west.

Eric's parents, a voice from deep within whispered to me. I looked around and noticed I was minutes away from Eric's parents' home in Conyers. I felt a surge of energy that propelled me to go to their house.

"There's no way. I can't just show up to those people's house. They will think I'm crazy," I reasoned. But the power would not wane. Instead it grew stronger and stronger, causing me to cry from being so overwhelmed by it.

"I can't do it!" I shouted.

You can do all things through Me who gives you strength.

I exhaled. I didn't want to make a fool of myself, but I finally felt God speaking clearly to me, giving me direction. I could not be defiant. Even if I obeyed, and I failed or looked stupid, at least I would be following His voice and not my own.

I turned off the highway at the next exit and proceeded to Eric's parents' house. I had no clue what I was going to say to them when I got there, but I would trust God for the right words.

I pulled up and saw both of his parents' cars sitting in the driveway. They were home. I was tempted to chicken out, to turn around, and drive away before they realized I was there.

Faith without works is dead. Trust Me.

I fearfully got out of the vehicle and made my way to the front door. I gulped before ringing the doorbell. I could hear the chime of the doorbell inside and then the shuffle of footsteps approaching the door.

The door swung open, but it was not Ernestine or Dwayne who answered. "Eric?" I looked at him puzzled.

"Amber? What are you doing here?" he asked just as quizzically as I had.

"I...I...Oh Lord, help me!" I started.

He gazed at my face and then stepped back. "Come in," he invited.

Tensely, I walked into the house and followed him into the living room. We sat down on the same sofa we'd been on during my prior visit. So much had changed since then.

"I'm sorry for just showing up like this. I don't usually just pop up at people's houses," I muttered in embarrassment.

"How did you know that I was here?"

I shook my head. "I didn't. I just felt that I was to come here. I can't explain it."

"I see." He sat back on the sofa, his face expressionless as if he were waiting for me to try to explain anyway.

I sucked in a deep breath. "Eric, I decided not to marry Gold. I gave him back his ring a few weeks ago. I also decided to forgo the Green Global deal. They weren't pleased about it, but I had to do what was right."

His face remained hardened. "I see. I'm sorry to hear about the engagement."

"I'm not. I couldn't marry him because of you."

He sat up. "Me?"

I nodded. "It wouldn't have been fair to him to marry him when my heart was with you. I would have never been able to give him all of me."

"What are you saying?" he asked, his face showing a mixture of anger and bewilderment.

Immediately, I knew what to say. I didn't know where the words came from, but they were there. "I know I hurt you, and for that I am terribly sorry. I was blind and dumb and letting everything distract me from what was most important. I used to think that when I met the man for me there would be birds chirping, and the sky would light up and everything would be magic. But you came and there were no birds, or lights, or magic involved. You just loved me and that was supposed to be enough. I was so busy looking for the extra stuff that I missed the blessing." I laughed, instantly being reminded of a story from the bible. "I guess I'm a lot like the Jews who had Jesus among them and refused to see that He was the Messiah. They were waiting for the extra too.

"Eric, I know I am asking for a lot to beg you to give me another chance, but I have been miserable without you. I need you in my world. I am my best when I'm with you."

He stared at me for several minutes. I wasn't sure if he was going to kiss me or tell me to leave. His face was emotionless. Uncomfortable with his gaze, I looked down at the floor.

"Amber, I want to hate you, but I can't. That's the thing about love, it overrides reason and logic. I wish you wouldn't have dated Gold behind my back or accepted his proposal in the first place, but had you not, I would have never known how deeply I care for you and how much you feel the same." He smiled for the first time since I had showed up. "Let's put ourselves out of our misery."

Before I could respond, he leaned over and kissed me. Fireworks like the Fourth of July! My heart was finally at home…

Valentine's Day the Following Year

Nine months later, I stood before God, my family, and friends and married my soul mate, Eric Hayes. Valentine's Day the previous year was the day he had shared his feelings for me so it was only fitting that we made that day our official anniversary. We decided to keep the wedding simple and have a standard church wedding with one hundred guests and then hold our reception at a local banquet hall. For the honeymoon, we were going to Jamaica! Ya Mon!

During the ceremony, we requested that we write our own pledges in addition to the customary religious vows. Eric looked so dapper in his white tuxedo that I almost forgot we were in public and slobbered him down. Ooh, I wanted to so badly, but I behaved…at least until he said his vows.

"Amber, the bible says that a virtuous wife is worth more than rubies," he began. "I wondered for many years if I would ever find a woman who was more valuable than any treasure I could find in this world. My question was answered the day I realized that my helpmeet was you. I love everything about you from your intelligence and inner beauty to your sexiness and outward glow. If my life ended tomorrow, I would be satisfied because God has given me a chance to know what it is like to love and be loved by someone imperfect, but perfect for me. I vow to you every day for the rest of my life to be a godly man who respects you, adores you, protects you, provides for you, and supports you. Let everyone in this room bear witness to my pledge and hold me accountable to this vow."

By the time he finished talking, I could barely see him through my watery eyes. That didn't stop me from reaching over, pulling him into my embrace, and kissing him with all of the pent up passion inside me. I probably would have never stopped had the preacher not cleared his throat and all one hundred of our guest had not burst into laughter.

Embarrassed by my temporary loss of control, I bit my lip and peeked at Eric who was grinning from ear to ear. Taking my turn, I passed my bouquet to my Maid of Honor, Tisha, took the microphone from Eric, and began my speech. "Eric, I cannot even begin to describe the joy that is in my heart. A fool looks a blessing in the face and walks away. I was that fool for so long. I am eternally grateful to God for sending such a wonderful man like you into my life. I know that with His help there is nothing that we can't overcome. For so long I wondered if this day would ever come, if I would ever know love and marriage and a family of my own. Well, today I finally see that all things truly work together for the good of those who love the Lord and are called according to His purpose. I am proud to take you as my husband, and I pray that I will be the kind of wife that helps you to become the best man that you can be. I submit myself to your leadership, I love you, and I trust you because I know that God abides within you."

I wiped the few tears that had fallen from Eric's eyes and smiled at him. Turning toward the audience, I made one last vow. "Everyone, there is one more item that we will be celebrating today." Tisha passed me a document sealed in a white envelope, and I held it up in the air. Eric looked at the envelope and then at me in shock, completely unaware of what I was doing. I heard shuffles and murmurs from the crowd, anticipating my next move.

"As you all know, I am the owner of three fairly successful businesses. One of those businesses is a real estate company called Amber Ross Realty in which Eric Hayes has worked for me as the office manager. Eric has been one of the best employees I have ever had, and it is because of his great business sense that the company is where it is today.

"Knowing that we were getting married, Eric intended to start looking for work elsewhere so that we didn't ruin our new marriage by mixing it with business. I have delayed his job search, bogging him down with busy work so that he didn't have time to apply elsewhere. We ended up agreeing that after the honeymoon he would restart his search.

"But he will not be restarting his job search because effective the moment the pastor pronounces us man and wife, Eric Hayes will be the new CEO of Hayes & Ross Realty formerly known as Amber Ross Realty. This envelope I am holding holds a document signing over my company to my husband and naming him as its new chief executive officer. Let me be the first to say, Congratulations Mr. Hayes!"

Applause broke out around the church, triggering an instant standing ovation. Eric stood there baffled; his bottom lip so low I thought it would touch the ground. Shaking himself out of his daze, he came over to me and gave me a big bear hug. "What? I can't believe this! Are you sure? Why?" he questioned.

"If we are going to be married, all that I have belongs to you and visa-versa. We can't go into this marriage with a 'his and hers' mentality. The bible says that the two become one. I already have a lot on my plate, and I have to make room for this marriage and hopefully one day kids. Who else would be a better choice to give my first business, my baby to than you? I trust you, and I believe in you."

The preacher took the microphone, had us exchange rings, and announced, "I now pronounce you man and wife. You may kiss your bride." And we kissed.

"Ladies and Gentlemen! It is my pleasure to introduce to you for the very first time, Mr. and Mrs. Eric Hayes!"

Epilogue

Lesson 31: To Everything There Is a Time

He has made everything beautiful in its time. (Ecclesiastes 3:11)

Three Months Later…

It has been twelve weeks since Eric and I wed, and I am more than sure that he was the right choice for me. He is gradually getting used to his new position as CEO of Hayes & Ross Realty, but I can tell he was meant for this and that he loves it. Since the wedding, I have continued to oversee the operations of Sweet Tooth Oasis and Sunrise Sunset Daycare. I have also implemented free training classes for women in parenting and business ownership on the Saturday mornings at the daycare. Lydia and I have been talking about offering the business classes at the church in the near future, but we have to get the approval of the Board of Trustees before we can begin planning.

Lydia informed me that because the overwhelming success of the first set of the Wife 101 and Husband 101 classes, the church has decided to offer the courses again this fall and maybe even continuing classes, Wife 202 and Husband 202, in the winter for those like me who have already completed the first course. There have also been some rumors about a couple's retreat, but I haven't heard anything confirming that it will happen. Eric is interested in taking the Husband class after hearing me talk about how much I learned during my class. The course starts in a few months, so we will just have to wait and see if he follows through.

I often replay last year's drama in my mind, analyzing my personal growth and how I got to the place that I am. When I enrolled in the Wife 101 course, I did it out of frustration and desperation, but I got so much more out of it than I bargained. God used the class to put a mirror up to me and allow me to see the real me. Regrettably, I had more flaws than I thought; however, through the process I have slowly begun to work on me. I'm still not a perfect woman, and I am no longer trying to be one. Instead, I am pressing towards developing the Fruits of the Spirit (love, joy, peace, patience, kindness, goodness, faithfulness, gentleness, and self-control) and letting the virtuous woman mentor me. I read Proverbs 31 weekly to remind myself of the kind of woman I aim to be. I know with the Lord's help, I'll get there eventually.

Just in case you are wondering what happened to the people in my life, here is a quick update. Gold and Perkins decided to continue on with the Green Global venture, using more of their own money to cover the loss of my investment. Last I heard there had been some leaks to the media about Green Global's shady endeavors, and the company may be under investigation. Tisha is still single and dating, looking for Mr. Right in all of the wrong places, but that's Tisha. My mom and stepfather are back in Long Island in their rebuilt home. We now keep in touch a few times a week and are planning to visit them over the summer. Chris and I have maintained our friendship. He has left Noel alone and is now dating someone he met at his job. I told him to be careful about those inner office romances. Like mine, they might end up at the alter!

Reading Group Guide

Amber's Story

1. Amber is told by her ex-boyfriend that she is too independent and does not allow him to play his role as a man in their relationship. Is there such a thing as being too independent? In today's society, have women and men become confused about gender roles?

2. Amber's best friend Tisha is very opinionated and influential as it relates to Amber's love life. Do you think this helps or hurts Amber? How do you decide whether the advice of friends should be taken or discarded?

3. Amber's personal struggles are linked back to her relationship with her mother and stepfather. How important was it for her to confront her past? Do you have any issues from your past that negatively affects your emotions and/or behaviors?

4. Amber dates three men: Chris, Gold, and Eric. Discuss the character of each man. Do you think she chose the right man in the end? Which one would you have chosen and why?

5. What are the changes that Amber has to make in her life to become a better woman who is more suited for marriage? Do you think change is necessary for a woman who desires to be married or to make her marriage work? Why or why not?

6. Instead of having chapters like most books, Wife 101 is organized by lessons. The lessons reflect the theme of that chapter and the lesson Amber gains about womanhood /wifehood. What did you think about the various lessons and the biblical reference connected to them? Are there any that stood out for you? Which lesson did you enjoy or learn from the most?

7. At the wedding, Amber gives her new husband her first business as a wedding present. Do you agree or disagree with this act of love and trust?

Why was it important for her to give him something so valuable? How can her act help or hurt her new marriage?

The Wife 101 Course: Proverbs 31

8. Which of the thirteen classes on the book of Proverbs was the most compelling? Why? What did you learn or how did it relate to your life?

9. The class is instructed to check off the qualities of a virtuous woman that they possess. Of the forty qualities listed in Lesson 28, how many of them do you possess? Which of them do you still need to develop? How can you work towards growing in these areas?

10. Lydia discusses the dilemma of time constraints and women working outside the home. Create an activity list of your own. Do you have enough time? What can you do to manage your time better? How do you feel about the impact of women in the workforce on family life?

11. Lydia stresses that a virtuous woman is committed to God, her family, and her community. Her behaviors, not her words, indicate this commitment. What do your behaviors indicate about your level of commitment to God, family, and community? How can you increase your devotion to these areas?

12. Proverbs 31:15 discusses a virtuous woman's prayer life and the preparations she makes for her family. Do you wake up early and pray or prepare for the day? In your opinion, how important is it to pray over your family and prepare them for their day? For one week, commit to waking up early, praying, and preparing. Afterwards, assess whether or not it made a difference in your day or week.

13. Proverbs 31:12 states that, "She comforts, encourages, and does him (her husband) only good as long as there is life within her." Does this reflect your relationship with your husband or significant other? Why is it so

difficult to measure up to this verse? What can you do to become a woman who avoids discouraging, discomforting, and doing her man badly?

14. Was there anything that surprised you about the study of Proverbs 31? Do you think that women should inspire to be like the virtuous woman?

Note from the Author

I began writing this novel after weeks upon weeks of studying Proverbs 31. Every morning I would get up and attempt to spend some quiet time with God, and each time He would send me to Proverbs 31. I would get so frustrated because I wanted to read something new and different, but He had a different plan for me. Over time, He revealed to me an understanding of the chapter that I never had before. I was amazed at how much wisdom about womanhood was hidden in these thirty-one verses and I knew I had to figure out a way to write about it and share this knowledge with the world. I first considered nonfiction, but I quickly recognized that I would be limiting myself to those who read nonfiction Christian literature, so I opted to build a fictional story around the teachings of Proverbs 31 in the hopes that the message would be accessible to more readers.

The main character, Amber Ross, is a mixture of every strong and independent woman that I know. She is a wonderful woman, but due to her acceptance of secular ideas, she is not the best candidate for wifehood or even motherhood. She defines herself way too much by her worldly success rather than her God-given purpose. She tries to control matters that are out of her control. And she thinks that being a wife is something you do after you have conquered everything else; not realizing that wifehood is synonymous of womanhood and a ministry created by God for His purpose and glory.

The three men in Amber's life (Gold, Chris, and Eric) represent the three common reasons why women marry. Gold reflects a marriage for financial stability and status. Chris embodies a marriage of convenience and comfort. Eric signifies a marriage built on faith in God and the embracing of marriage as a ministry. Other characters also have symbolic meanings such as Tisha, the well-meaning friend who gives bad advice, Lydia, the mentor and counselor who is a constant reminder of God's way of doing things, and Anita and Otis, the people and experiences from the past that influence our fears and struggles.

It is my prayer that after reading this book, it is not just another story to you, but that you take something positive away from it that you can add to your life. As Amber surrenders her dreams and plans to the Lord, understand that He wants the same from you. I would love to hear your feedback and questions so please review the novel on Amazon or other book review sites and/or email me at drajwilson@gmail.com. Also, be on the lookout for the sequel to this book, *Husband 101*...The story has just begun...Happy Reading!

A'ndrea J. Wilson

www.andreawilsononline.com

Photograph by Antonio Cleveland

A'ndrea J. Wilson, Ph.D. is the author of both fiction and nonfiction books, including the novel, *The Things We Said We Would Never Do,* and the devotional, *My Business His Way: Wisdom & Inspiration for Entrepreneurs.* She holds a Bachelor's of Science in Psychology, a Master's of Science in Counseling Psychology; Marriage and Family Therapy, and a Doctorate in Global Leadership; Educational Leadership. A'ndrea works as a college professor, as well as conducts workshops on a variety of personal and professional topics. Dr. Wilson is the Founder and President of Divine Garden Press, a publishing company that specializes in fiction and nonfiction books addressing marriage and family issues. She is a member of Zeta Phi Beta Sorority, Inc. and is frequently involved in community service activities. A native of Rochester, New York, she currently resides in Georgia. Please visit her online at www.andreawilsononline.com or email her at drajwilson@gmail.com.

Other Books by A'ndrea J. Wilson

Nonfiction

My Business His Way: Wisdom & Inspiration for Entrepreneurs

Kiss & Tell: Releasing Expectations

Fiction

The Things We Said We Would Never Do

Ready & Able Teens: Ebony's Bad Habit

Ready & ABLE Teens: Desiree Dishes the Dirt (Spring 2012)